'I'm sorry,' Ben said softly. 'This must be really upsetting for you.'

For a moment or two Sarah gave in to the wonderful feeling of comfort that his nearness evoked. His head rested against hers, and she absorbed the warmth that came from being near him. His arms were strong and capable, and she was sure that he meant what he said, that he would lift any burden from her, given the chance.

When **Joanna Neil** discovered Mills & Boon®, her life-long addiction to reading crystallised into an exciting new career writing Medical™ Romance. Her characters are probably the outcome of her varied lifestyle, which includes working as a clerk, typist, nurse and infant teacher. She enjoys dressmaking and cooking at her Leicestershire home. Her family includes a husband, son and daughter, an exuberant yellow Labrador and two slightly crazed cockatiels. She currently works with a team of tutors at her local education centre, to provide creative writing workshops for people interested in exploring their own writing ambitions.

Recent titles by the same author:

HIS VERY SPECIAL BRIDE

BY
JOANNA NEIL

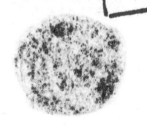

MILLS & BOON®

Pure reading pleasure™

First published in Great Britain 2008
Harlequin Mills & Boon Limited,
Eton House, 18-24 Paradise Road, Richmond, Surrey TW9 1SR

© Joanna Neil 2008

ISBN: 978 0 263 19908 6

Set in Times Roman 10½ on 13 pt
15-0808-52592

Printed and bound in Great Britain
by Antony Rowe Ltd, Chippenham, Wiltshire

HIS VERY
SPECIAL BRIDE

CHAPTER ONE

'ARE you quite sure that you want to do this?' Carol Farley laid a hand lightly on Sarah's shoulder, her grey eyes skimming her face with a hint of anxiety. 'I can't help thinking that you're not ready to make it on your own in the world just yet. You do know that we're happy for you to stay here with us for just as long as you want, don't you?'

'I know.' Sarah managed a smile. 'You and Tom have both been so good to me, and I want you to know that I appreciate all that you've done, both for me and for Emily. It's just that if I don't step out now and try to manage on my own, I don't think I'll ever pluck up the courage to do it. I feel that I have to get back to a normal kind of life…whatever that might be.'

'But it hasn't been all that long since you came out of hospital…just a matter of a few months…and I'm sure you need more time to adjust.' Carol frowned. 'You suffered a nasty head injury, and even now there are things that you struggle with. How are you going to cope, especially with a small child in tow?'

'It's been six months at least…and it's high time that I started to manage things for myself. Somehow, I'll find a way.' Sarah pulled in a deep, steadying breath and glanced across the sunlit kitchen to where Emily was playing with a doll's house in a far corner of the dining area. She was nearly three years old, and was just beginning to break out of the subdued state she had been in not too long ago. 'I have to.'

The little girl was chattering softly to a small, golden-haired doll that she was walking in and out of the rooms of the house. 'We have to cook dinner,' she said in a piping voice. 'Put the saucepan on the cooker.' Then she looked up at Sarah and added with a chuckle, 'Mummy, look...Dolly's holding the saucepan.'

'So she is.' Sarah smiled, her gaze remaining on her daughter as Emily turned back to her game.

She was a pretty girl, with silky blonde hair that curled softly into the nape of her neck and fell in wispy tendrils around her temples.

Unconsciously, Sarah pushed back a lock of her own honey blonde hair that had fallen across her cheek, tucking the spiralling strand behind her ear.

At the hospital they had told her that Emily was her child, and certainly she loved her dearly, the bond between them growing stronger day by day. It was just that nothing in her life made sense to her any more, and she felt as though she was trapped in a place where all was chaos and confusion.

Her hair had grown to shoulder length since that fateful day when she had been injured, and it seemed strange to her that she had such a wild mass of unruly curls. But, then, every feature seemed strange to her in the mirror.

'Do you mind watching Emily for me while I go and look over the cottage?' Sarah said now, turning to look at the woman who had been her mainstay over these last few months. 'I could take her with me, if you like.'

'No, you don't want to be doing that.' The older woman's response was firm. 'You'll want to check things out without any distractions. Of course she'll be all right with me.' Carol gave a faint smile, her motherly features creasing lightly, but there was a glimmer of sadness in her eyes. 'She's still my foster-child, after all.'

Perhaps there was a hint of anguish in the words, or maybe it was resignation that Sarah heard. Whatever it was, it caused her to glance afresh at the older woman, a troubled look in her eyes.

'Are you afraid that you'll lose her? I know how much you've come to love Emily.' Her voice softened, and she reached out a hand to touch Carol's arm. It suddenly seemed important to do what she could to reassure this woman who had become her friend over the last few months. 'I will take good care of her, you know, and, whatever happens about the cottage, we won't be going far away. I'll bring her back to see you, and you'll always be welcome to come and visit.'

Carol slipped her arms around her and gave her a hug. 'Yes, I know you will, and I'm glad of that. Take no notice of me. You've been like a daughter to me, and I worry too much, I know I do. I just wish that you had been able to recover your memory, or at least some portion of it, before now. That would have made me feel more certain that you were ready to take on this move.'

'I'll be fine,' Sarah murmured. She straightened, preparing herself. 'Physically, at least, there's nothing wrong with me, and this is something that I need to do, for myself and Emily.' She fingered the key in her pocket. 'I have the key from the estate agent, so I'll head over to the house right away and see if it has everything that I need. Don't worry about me.

It's just that I have to do this for myself—a first stab at independence, if you like.'

Carol nodded. 'I can see that you've made up your mind, and I won't stand in your way. I just hope that you'll remember that we're always here for you.'

'I will.' Sarah smiled and then went over to the little girl, crouching down beside her and saying lightly, 'I have to go out for a little while, Emily, but Auntie Carol will look after you. Will you be a good girl for her while I'm gone?'

''Course I will.' Emily gave her a bright smile, her blue eyes reflecting the colour of Sarah's gentle gaze.

'Love you,' Sarah said, giving the child a kiss, and then she stood up and turned away, going in search of her bag.

The drive to the cottage didn't take long, but as the countryside swept by, Sarah had time to reflect on how easily the skill of driving had come back to her, as though it was second nature to her. The local authority had made special provision for her to take her test under the name that she was now using, and once she had passed she had been able to pick up this little runabout for next to nothing. It had been one more step on the way to getting her life back.

The hamlet where she had been living these last few months nestled in a green valley, set between the rolling hills that formed the southern tip of the Pennine range. All around there was lush vegetation, heather-clad moorland and trees whose branches swayed in the gentle summer breeze. Here and there she caught a glimpse of a river in the distance, the sunlight glinting on the surface of the water so that it looked like a ribbon of silver winding its way through the verdant meadowland.

After a while, Sarah turned the car off the country road into a narrow lane that led towards two isolated properties.

Approaching the small cottage, she drew the car to a halt on the gravelled forecourt and gazed around her. This had to be the right place. There was a wall plaque that read BRIDGE END COTTAGE.

She slid out of the car and went to take a closer look. Everywhere was silent, deserted looking, and there were no other cars to be seen. Perhaps whoever lived in the neighbouring house was out at work.

She let her glance trail over the adjacent property. It was a grand affair, well kept and truly impressive, with a steeply sloping roof and dormer windows and an attractive single-storey extension to the main building. She gave a faint sigh. Unfortunately, that wasn't the house she was here to look at.

She turned her attention back to Bridge End Cottage and frowned. There was a general air of neglect around the stone-built house, and the shrubs that scrambled against the front wall were overgrown and unkempt. It wasn't at all what she had expected to see after the brief, enthusiastic summary the estate agent had given her.

'You're really fortunate,' he had said. 'The cottage has only just come into our hands, and we haven't put the details out on the market yet. You'll be the first to view it, and I'm sure it will suit your needs down to the ground. The rent's not too high, it's compact, with a garage on the side, and there's a mature garden at the back.'

Sarah wasn't sure what the rest of the house would reveal, but she could see right away that the garage roof was in need of repair. Some of the tiles were missing, and it looked as though there was a tear in the roofing felt. As to the main building, it was clear that the window-frames hadn't seen a lick of paint in a long, long time.

She steeled herself to go and take a look at the rest of the property. It was small wonder that the rent was so low, but could she afford to be picky? Did she really have much choice about what she could take on when her budget was limited, to say the least?

She walked over to the porch and tried her key in the lock, but when she attempted to turn it, nothing happened. It wouldn't budge. Frustrated, she took it out and examined to see if it was damaged in some way. It wasn't, as far as she could tell, so she tried again.

Still nothing. She ground her teeth in silent frustration. Had the agent given her the wrong key? He had been pushed for time, and certainly he had appeared to be distracted by other customers walking into the office, all of which had left her with this dilemma. The last thing she wanted was to have to go all the way into town to pick up another one.

Maybe she could take a look around the back of the house and peer in through the windows? At least that would give her some idea of what the place had to offer.

She pushed open the wooden side gate, wincing as it creaked on its hinges in protest, and went through to the garden at the back of the house. Her eyes widened as she looked around. The estate agent's jargon had termed it mature, but that had been an understatement. This was a jungle, an overgrowth of rampant shrubs and tangled trees. It had obviously been a long while since any work had been done in this garden.

Turning her attention towards the house, Sarah tried the back door and found that it was locked. Then, as she stood considering her options, her gaze brightened a fraction. There was a window open on the ground floor, and that brought all

kinds of possibilities to mind. She was slender enough to
wriggle her way through it if she could climb up on something and reach up as far as the sill. After all, it wouldn't be
breaking and entering, would it, or even trespass, as she had
permission to be here and view the property?

The thought was no sooner in her mind than she was acting
on it. An overturned metal bucket made a handy step, and in
the blink of an eye she had clambered up and was aiming to
slide through the narrow window space. The pocket of her
denim jeans snagged on the latch that jutted from the sill, and
she halted for a moment or two, trying to free herself.

The bucket fell with a clatter, but she ignored the commo-
tion and after a moment she continued to squirm through the
gap. The window opened into a kitchen, and the sink unit was
handily placed for her to ease herself into the room.

Success was just a breath away. One more thrust of her hips
and she would be in.

'Can I help you in any way?' The firm male voice cut into
the silence like the smooth crack of a whip, and Sarah froze.

Where had he come from? Whoever he was, he didn't
sound as though he was at all ready to lend a helping hand.
Just the opposite, in fact.

'Uh…I don't think so,' she murmured, stuck in the incon-
gruous position of being caught half in and half out of the
window, with her back to the intruder.

'Really? Only you seem to be having some difficulty
getting into the property. It occurs to me that the reason for
that could be that you aren't following the normal procedure.
Most people would prefer to make use of the door.'

'Yes. That's very true.' She started to twist around, easing
herself into a sitting position. 'I wonder what on earth could

have made me think that going through the window would be easier?' Cautiously, she let her fingers lightly rest on the window-frame so that she could keep her balance.

Her sarcasm was clearly lost on him, because he answered smoothly, 'Those were my thoughts exactly. I have to say it occurred to me that there's the advantage of not being seen from the front of the house.' He paused. 'Of course, that's assuming you don't kick buckets over and make your where-abouts known.'

Her gaze flicked downwards in the direction of the voice, and she found herself looking at a pair of long legs encased in olive-green chinos. Letting her glance sweep upwards, she saw that her interrogator was flat stomached, and that his chest, covered by an expensively tasteful linen shirt, broad-ened out to complement a pair of wide, capable-looking shoulders. His body was fit, honed to lean perfection, and even before her eyes had reached his face and meshed with his dark, piercing gaze, the breath had snagged in her throat.

Good looking was not an apt description. She swallowed hard. He was awesome, and well worth a second glance, if only she hadn't been diverted by the way he was standing there, calmly assessing her, his grey eyes glimmering with a brooding expression that she found hard to fathom.

She managed to find her voice once more. Breathing evenly to keep her composure, she said, 'Actually, you don't need to concern yourself about me being here. I know it must look odd, but there is a perfectly reasonable explanation.'

'I'm glad to hear it,' he said. 'Perhaps you'd care to en-lighten me?'

'Yes, of course.' She frowned. Surely he wasn't the owner of the property, who had come back to take a last look around?

No one with his muscular build and general look of vitality would have left the place to fall into ruin, would they? She said carefully, 'I have the wrong key. I mean, I thought I had the right key, but something's wrong with it.'

'Hmm. I can see how that would be a problem.' His gaze narrowed on her, and she had the strong impression that he believed she was making it up as she went along. 'Perhaps you should let me help you down from there and we might be able to find a way to sort this out.'

Sarah gave him a direct look. 'Is that possible? Do you have a key?'

His mouth made a wry slant. 'You're not one to give up, are you? First things first…let's start with me helping you down from there, shall we?'

She frowned, torn between ignoring him and gaining entry in her own way, and on the other hand acquiescing to his request. But since this man obviously didn't intend going anywhere until she complied, she really didn't have any choice but to follow his bidding. If she went on with her attempt to gain access to the house, it was more than likely that he would simply call the police, even though anyone could see that she wasn't a burglar, couldn't they?

'I think I can manage by myself, thanks all the same.' The bucket had long since rolled away and that would make her descent a trifle more precarious, but she wasn't going to let that hamper her. She began to ease herself down from the window-sill and prepared to jump the last bit of the way.

He forestalled her, though, before her feet had even left the bulwark of the wall, reaching out to her and splaying his hands around her waist, so that she felt herself being lifted from her vantage point. Holding her close by using his long body as support, he allowed her to slide gently down the last couple of feet to the ground, leaving her humiliatingly aware of the taut proximity of his muscled length as her feminine curves were softly held against him.

Steadying her as her feet finally touched the ground, he waited for what seemed like endless moments before he gently released her. Sarah didn't know where to look. She was having strange difficulty with her breathing, and her face must surely be flushed from that close encounter. She wasn't at all confident that she wanted to look him in the eye just then.

'Are you OK?' His voice drifted over her, a deep rumbling sound that had her skin tingling in response. He was altogether too male, and far too close for comfort for her peace of mind.

'I'm fine,' she murmured, trying to shake off the sensation of heat that his touch had evoked in her, and which even now was racing out of control through her bloodstream. It was a distraction that she could do without, but one that nevertheless persisted in clouding her mind.

'If you're sure about that,' he said, 'perhaps you could tell me what you're doing here?'

She looked up at him then, a hint of annoyance flashing in her blue eyes. 'I would have thought that was fairly obvious,' she retorted. 'I want to look around the house. What did you think I had in mind—an attempt to make off with the antiques?'

He inclined his head a fraction. 'I have to admit that thought had crossed my mind. Alfred left some valuable bits and pieces in the house when he went into hospital, and I promised him that I would pack them up and send them on to his family. I've been too busy of late to finish the job, but I planned on crating up the last few items today.'

Sarah's jaw dropped. 'I didn't realise… I mean…I had no idea that there were any such things in the house.' She pressed her lips together momentarily and then added in a husky tone, 'Look, do you think we could start again? This is not at all what it must appear. I really do have a key that the estate agent gave me, but I think he must have mixed it up with one for another property. Perhaps the numbers are the same, or maybe there's a Bridge End Road somewhere.'

He studied her thoughtfully for a second or two, his grey gaze flicking over her, and she looked away, feeling awkward. Then pride came to her rescue and she braced herself to deal with the situation. Why should she feel guilty for simply trying to counter the estate agent's mistake?

Dragging her eyes back to his tall frame a moment later, she forced herself to meet his gaze.

To her surprise, he nodded. 'You're probably right.'

Sarah gave a soft sigh of relief. Was he finally accepting that she wasn't an intruder? His expression was noncommittal, though, and she studied him closely, trying to work out what might be going on in his mind. It was a doomed effort, and after a moment her thoughts wandered idly. She couldn't help but notice how well the short-cropped cut of his midnight-black hair suited him. It seemed somehow at one with his strongly defined features, the angular jaw and the straight line of his brows.

He said crisply, 'I dare say there must have been a mistake somewhere along the way…only the property wasn't supposed to be going on the market for another couple of days. By then I would have finished with the clearing up.'

Sarah's attention came back with a jerk. 'Yes, the agent did tell me that they weren't quite ready…but he didn't seem to be at all concerned about me coming to look the place over.'

'That doesn't surprise me at all.' His mouth made a crooked shape. 'The cottage is in such bad condition that they'll probably struggle to find a tenant. I wouldn't have thought many people would want to take it on, and Alfred's family haven't yet managed to find a buyer.'

A small line indented her brow. 'Has something happened to Alfred? You said that he went into hospital.' All at once Sarah found herself concerned with the fate of the poor man who had been too ill to maintain his property and who'd had to abandon all his worldly goods to another's care. 'You're a friend of his?'

'Neighbour. I live next door. I used to call round to make sure that he was all right. Then, one day, I found him in a state of collapse after he'd had a fall. It turned out that his heart had gone into an abnormal rhythm, causing him to black out for a short time. He cracked a rib as he fell against the side-board and he wasn't able to get up again.'

Sarah sucked in a quick breath. 'Had he been lying there for a long while?'

He shook his head. 'A matter of minutes, I believe. I think he was just about to prepare for bed when he became ill. Luckily, I was on a late shift that day, and when I came home happened to check on him.'

'So you called for an ambulance and waited with him?'

He nodded. 'I did. It wasn't too long before the para-medics arrived.'

She tried to imagine how she would have coped under those circumstances. 'Even so, that must have been nerve-racking wait.'

'From the point of view of a friend wanting to lend a helping hand, yes, it was, but I'm a doctor, so at least I knew what to do to stabilise his condition. I had my medical bag to hand, fortunately.'

'A doctor…' Sarah studied him all over again. Perhaps that accounted for his calm, confident manner, both in his handling of Alfred's crisis and in his way of dealing with finding a potential trespasser on the premises. It was beginning to look as though this man was a force to be reckoned with.

'And how is he now? Did he pull through?' It hadn't been all that long ago since Sarah herself had been in a desperate, helpless situation, and she could readily identify with the injured man. She had no idea who it was who had attacked her and left her fighting for her life, but someone had come along and rescued her, just as this man had done for Alfred.

'He did.' He made a brief smile. 'He's OK, but he's not well enough to live on his own any longer. His family live some distance away, down in Somerset, and I don't think they realised how frail he was until I called them.'

'So, are they taking care of him now?'

'Yes, they are.' He glanced around. 'As to the cottage, Alfred has a sentimental attachment to the place, but he's leaving it up to his family to sort things out. I believe they would like to sell, but they decided to put it up for rent while they make up their minds. Not that anyone is likely to take it on, given the state it's in.'

'Well, you never know, do you? Perhaps I could take a look around?' Sarah ventured. 'I really need to find somewhere to live.'

He frowned. 'I doubt very much that this will be what you

want, but certainly I can let you into the house. I'm Ben, by the way. Ben Brinkley.'

'Sarah…Hall.' She hesitated over the words that still seemed strange to her. She had no idea who she really was, but the name Sarah had been on the tip of her tongue when they'd asked her at the hospital, and from the outset, as young as she was, Emily had called herself Emily Hall. So that was the name that had stuck. Despite all the attempts that had been made to track Sarah's origins, though, none had revealed anything of who she was and where she had come from.

He reached into his pocket and took out a key, inserting it into the lock of the back door. 'If you take my advice, you'll look elsewhere. I've been opening the windows to air the place, but I suspect there's a problem with damp, and I don't think anyone's going to be dealing with it any time soon. I arranged for someone to come and put in a new fire for Alfred in the living room, so that he could be warm at least, and I've decorated the main bedroom and replaced the rotting window-frame in there, but there's a limit to how much I've been able to do, given the hours I work.' He pushed open the door to the kitchen and waved a hand for her to go inside.

Sarah walked into the room, and her spirits sank as soon as she looked around. It seemed as though the kitchen hadn't been touched since the turn of the previous century, with battered stand-alone cupboards lining the walls and a plain, rectangular wooden table in the middle of the room. The north-facing wall showed patches of damp, extending along its length. As for any means of cooking, there was a rusty old range up against one wall. She frowned. 'I wonder how Alfred managed to cook his meals.'

'I think he mostly relied on the microwave to heat things

up,' Ben said, 'or he would come round to my place to share a meal with me.'

Sarah smiled. 'It sounds as though you were a good neighbour to him.'

Ben gave a negligent shrug. 'I did what I could.' He glanced around. 'Let me show you the rest of the place. It won't take long, because there's only the kitchen and living room downstairs, and just the two dormer bedrooms and a small bathroom upstairs. It's all very much on a par with what you see down here.'

He sounded as though he thought the tour was a waste of time, and Sarah gave him a quick sidelong look. Why was he so sure that she wouldn't want to live here?

'Are you hoping to put me off?' she queried lightly.

He pushed open the door to the living room. 'I think the house will do that all by itself,' he said. His glance skimmed over her. 'Besides, you're as slender as a string bean and you don't look as though you have the wherewithal to tackle the work that would be needed to put things right.'

Sarah made a face at that. His comment about her slender shape had struck home. People had remarked on how slim she was. Perhaps it had been the time she had spent in hospital and the confusion as to who she was and what had happened to her that had made her lose weight. The clothes she had been wearing when she had been found no longer fitted her, but hung on her slender frame.

She stiffened her shoulders. All that was going to change. She was determined to make a new start, if only for Emily's sake.

'Isn't that the landlord's responsibility?'

'Maybe, but it's unlikely that Alfred's family will be doing any renovations in the short term. Their responsibilities end with matters of health and safety…things like making sure that the appliances are in sound condition.'

So any changes to make the place comfortable would be left to the tenant, assuming that permission was given. Sarah pressed her lips together, absorbing that fact before she started to look around.

The living room was drab, in need of decorating, and the heavy curtains tended to block out the light, lending a sombre air to the place. On the plus side, there were one or two small pieces of furniture that pointed to someone with a collector's eye, and she noted a cabinet housing several antiques that wouldn't have been out of place in a fine country mansion.

Upstairs, the main bedroom was clean and comfortable, with softly patterned walls and freshly painted woodwork, though the second bedroom was in a sorry state. The floor covering was brittle and cracked, and the paper on the walls was yellowed with age. Poor Alfred must have been in desperate need of help until Ben had come along.

'The bathroom isn't too bad. It's a bit cramped, but at least the plumbing is in order.' Ben showed her into the room and then waited outside on the landing while she took a look around.

The bath was Victorian in style, with clawed feet and chipped enamel, and, as he had said, there was very little room to spare. Sarah suspected that what had once been a large bathroom had been divided to allow for a second bedroom.

'Thank you for showing me around,' she said, as they started down the narrow stairs. 'I do appreciate you taking the time. I'll have to call in on the estate agent tomorrow and tell him about the mix-up.'

'I expect he already knows. Like you said, someone

looking at a Bridge End Road property is probably wondering right now why his key isn't working.'

Back in the kitchen, Sarah took a last look around. None of what she had seen filled her with enthusiasm, and perhaps that showed in her expression because Ben said, 'Don't think of it as a waste of time, but more as a guide to comparing properties in the future. You've gained an idea of what there is at the bottom of the heap.'

He walked with her out into the garden and turned to lock the door. 'Better luck next time.'

She sent him an oblique glance. 'You're very sure that I won't be coming back, aren't you? Are you going to be this way with all your potential neighbours, or are you hoping that the place will stay empty?'

'Now, there's an appealing thought,' he said in a musing tone. 'I could enjoy the tranquillity of a country retreat, with nothing to disturb me except for the birdsong every morning. I think I might work on that some more, and maybe I'll be able to come up with a plan of action.'

Sarah might have believed that he was joking if it hadn't been for the pensive flicker that stirred in the depths of his grey eyes. Maybe he was something of a loner, content to spend his leisure time in solitary comfort.

Either way, he was already walking her back to her car, and she guessed that for him the incident was over and done with. He would see her on her way, and then retreat to his peaceful hideaway.

As for Sarah, she had a decision to make. Would the cottage make a suitable home for Emily? And how would the doctor take to having a lively child around the place? Not too well, she would imagine, if he really valued a quiet life.

CHAPTER TWO

A GENTLE smile touched Sarah's lips as she gazed down at the sleeping child. Emily's honey-coloured curls were splayed out over the pillow, her golden lashes brushing the softness of her cheeks. Her tiny hands held the bedspread lightly as she began to stir.

'Emily, sunbeam, it's time to wake up.' Sarah stroked her daughter's silky hair and Emily's eyelids fluttered open.

She rubbed the sleep from her eyes with her fists and then lifted her arms up to Sarah, winding them around her neck. 'Am I going to nursery today?'

'Yes.' Sarah gave her a kiss and a hug. 'I'm going to take you there as soon as we've had breakfast. That will be good, won't it? You'll be able to play with the other children.'

Emily scrunched up her nose. 'I want to go in the little cars. Joseph pusheded me out the way last time and the teacher told him off.' She frowned. 'Will we be able to go outside?'

Sarah smiled. 'I expect so. It's a beautiful day today, so you'll probably be playing outside for quite a lot of the time. And I'm sure the teacher will be looking out for Joseph, to make sure that he takes his turn along with everyone else.'

Emily smiled contentedly. 'Don't want that T-shirt,' she

said, pointing to the pile of clothes that Sarah had laid out ready. 'I want the pink one with the shiny writing.'

'Oh, you do, do you, madam?' Sarah put her head on one side, looking on with amusement as the little girl scrambled out of bed. 'And I suppose you want the pink hair slides as well, do you?'

The child nodded and scampered into the bathroom, leaving Sarah to follow. 'Well, I dare say we can do that,' Sarah murmured. 'Let's see how we get on with you washing and dressing yourself, shall we? Perhaps you can manage to pull your top on all by yourself today.'

'I can.' Emily's voice rose with astonishment. 'I can do it. Mummy forgot.'

Sarah laughed. 'Perhaps I did. You'll have to show me all over again.' She knew very well that Emily was beginning to manage her clothes for herself, but even so she had to acknowledge that it wasn't unusual for her to have trouble recalling the small everyday things that cropped up. There were still times when she felt confused, as though her mind was playing tricks on her.

She was getting better every day, though, and yesterday's visit to the cottage had been something of a landmark achievement, albeit that it had been marred by her unexpected meeting with the good-looking doctor.

What must he have made of her? He probably thought that she was a strange young woman with a decidedly nonconformist manner. Then again, she had at least managed to recover her composure, and she had been able to talk to him as though her actions were perfectly normal.

Even Carol had to admit that she was stronger in all ways... Sarah frowned. All but the one that really counted.

It was a fact that she still didn't know who she was, and her past remained a mystery to her. Much as she loved her daughter, it still seemed alien to her to have discovered that she was the mother of this beautiful child. These last few months had been like a rebirth, in every sense, and each day that passed brought with it new challenges.

'See, Mummy? I done it myself.' Emily shrugged into her T-shirt and beamed at Sarah, bringing her out of her reverie.

'So you have. Clever girl.'

After breakfast, Sarah gathered up her bag in readiness for the day ahead, and then started to look around for her notebook. Her brow furrowed. She was sure that she had put it somewhere safe, in a place where she would easily find it.

'Have you lost something?' Carol asked. Emily's foster-mother was stacking crockery in the dishwasher, but now she stopped what she was doing in order to glance quizzically across the kitchen in Sarah's direction.

'My notepad,' Sarah murmured. 'I thought I had left it on the top of the sideboard, but it isn't there.'

'I saw you sliding it into your document wallet last night,' Carol said. 'You said that you had finished writing your pieces for the local newspaper and you would drop them in to the office today when you went into town to see the estate agent.'

'Of course I did.' Sarah slapped a hand to her forehead. 'I thought it would be easier if I kept everything together.' She sighed. 'I should have written myself a memo and stuck it on the fridge.'

Carol smiled. 'Not to worry. You're getting there, little by little.'

Sarah's mouth made a crooked slant. 'At least it's not just me having problems if the mishap over the key is anything to go by.'

'That's true. The estate agent must have had a momentary lapse.' Carol hesitated, sending her a thoughtful glance. 'So, are you still set on taking on the cottage?'

Sarah nodded. 'It isn't in the best of shape, but I don't see that I have any choice. It's about all that I can afford until my job prospects improve—my freelance writing is beginning to bring in a modest income, but it isn't enough to provide a terrific standard of living. At least the effort I'll have to put in to make the cottage into a home will be good therapy for me.' She frowned. 'I just hope that Social Services won't decide that it's not a fit place for Emily.'

'I doubt they'll object. After all, from the sound of it, there isn't anything too untoward about the property, apart from some damp in the kitchen. Besides, having a doctor living next door might turn out to be an advantage.'

Sarah made a face. 'I don't think he'll see it quite that way. The impression I had was that he would much prefer to be left to himself and, to be honest, that actually suits me right down to the ground. I need some space so that I can clear my head.'

'Not too much space, I hope?' Carol was frowning. 'I know you want to take on more work, and that you're determined to go it alone, but you have to think of Emily in all this. She's been through a lot, with you being away in hospital for a time, and the last thing she needs is for you to suffer a relapse. That's why you have to remember that I'm here for you, for both of you.'

Sarah clasped her hand and gave it a gentle squeeze. 'I will. Like I said, I'm not going to be far away, and we'll be back to pester you on a regular basis.'

'That will be fine by me.' Carol's face creased into a smile.

'Did the neighbour say where it was that he worked? Perhaps he's a GP, with a practice nearby. That would be handy for you and Emily, wouldn't it?'

Sarah felt a rush of heat ripple through her at the mere thought. Ben Brinkley as her GP? Heaven forbid. Even now she could remember with startling clarity the feel of his long body brushing against hers as he had helped her. Her whole system had gone into overdrive.

'I don't think I would be in any hurry to sign up on his list,' she said on a husky note. She could well imagine that her blood pressure would soar sky high just as soon as she stepped into any surgery run by him. 'I'd much rather settle for a more genial, fatherly type.' She frowned. 'Anyway, he was at home in the middle of a weekday afternoon, so I doubt he's in general practice. Maybe he works shifts at the local hospital.'

That would make living near to him easier to handle, from her point of view. After all, it meant that he would probably be working some weekends, and that would narrow down the risk of her running into him, wouldn't it?

A short time later, after she had dropped Emily off at nursery school, Sarah drove into the local town. Parking her car, she walked across the cobbled square, and headed for the estate agent's office.

'I'm so sorry about the trouble you had,' the young man said, getting up from behind his desk and coming towards her. 'I must have put the wrong label on the key. It was lucky for you that the neighbour happened to be around yesterday when you visited the property.'

Sarah stared at him. 'I remember ringing you to tell you about the mix-up,' she said, 'but how did you know about the neighbour? I don't recall telling you about him.'

'No…no, he rang me.' His expression was something between apologetic and awkward. 'I think he wanted to check that you were who you said you were. The property wasn't meant to have been put on the market for another day or so and he wasn't expecting anybody to be viewing it.'

Sarah winced. Dr Brinkley was certainly thorough in his way of getting to the bottom of things. He'd obviously had doubts about her version of events and somehow that didn't seem to bode well for their forthcoming relationship as neighbours.

'But the cottage is still up for rent, isn't it?'

'Oh, yes, it is.' His face brightened. 'Are you interested in taking up the tenancy, then?'

'I am. Do you have some papers for me to sign?'

He nodded. 'Yes, yes…I'll sort them out right away.' Clearly, he was eager to finalise things before she had the opportunity to change her mind, and just a few minutes later Sarah left the office. In her bag, she had the correct set of keys, and all the necessary documentation for her new tenancy.

Was this the beginning of a new life? The thought was a little daunting, but at least she had made a start. Straightening her shoulders, she began to walk along the street, heading in the direction of the offices of the local newspaper.

'Oh, no… Stop…stop… Slow down…' A woman's voice rang out, shrill with desperation, and she put up a hand as though to indicate that someone should stop. The woman was walking towards her, looking beyond Sarah to a point behind her. Sarah's purposeful stride slowed to a halt and she glanced behind her to see what was happening.

A motorcyclist was slowing down, indicating that he wanted to turn right at a junction, and he had positioned himself in the centre of the road. All appeared to be well, except that in the background there was the aggressive, speeding drone of an oncoming car.

Sarah turned round fully to take a better look. On the brow of the hill, she saw that a driver of a black saloon was overtaking on a bend in the road, and he was heading straight for the motorcyclist. The woman who had been shouting was gesticulating now, miming a frantic warning, but Sarah was very much afraid that it had come too late.

At the last moment the man behind the wheel of the car seemed to realise what was about to happen. He wrenched the steering-wheel, swerving to the left as he tried to avoid the motorbike, but he was going too fast and it was clear to Sarah that his actions were too late.

She watched in horror as he hit the bike with the front wing of his car and then smashed into another driver who was innocently heading straight on in the left-hand lane of the road. The front of the black saloon crumpled like a concertina and the car that had been hit swung round violently.

Sarah ran towards the mangled cars and the bike, anxious to do what she could to help.

To her dismay, she saw that the motorcyclist was lying on his side, his leg trapped beneath the bulk of his motorcycle. He appeared to be unconscious, but after a swift check she discovered that his airway was clear and he was still breathing, albeit faintly.

Instinctively, she reached for her phone. 'Emergency services—I need an ambulance,' she said, her breath coming in short gasps as she realised the enormity of the situation.

'Will you help me to lift the bike off him?' Sarah flung the question at a man who had come to stare at the devastation all around.

'Of course.' Together they freed the young man from the weight of the vehicle that was trapping him, and Sarah knelt down to check him over more thoroughly.

The woman who had been shouting earlier appeared to be in a panic, flapping her arms wildly and running about as though she was unsure what to do next.

'Do you think you could try to stop the oncoming traffic?' Sarah suggested briefly. She could see that the biker had a thigh wound, with blood seeping through his jeans, and now she laid the heel of her hand on to his thigh and applied pressure. 'Perhaps you could position yourself over the brow of the hill to stop anyone from coming any closer,' she told the woman, 'but make sure that you stay on the pavement.'

The woman nodded, and Sarah guessed she was glad to be able to do something useful. The man who had assisted her must have decided that was the best option, too, because he went with the woman, saying, 'You take the near side to the brow of the hill, and I'll go further along, to slow them down.'

Another man was already heading across the far side of the road to halt the traffic there.

Sarah took off her light cotton jacket and folded it up, making it into a tight wad. Then she whipped the leather belt from the waistband of her jeans and used it to strap the wad in place over the man's thigh, close to the source of bleeding.

After that, she hurried over to the other two vehicles and she quickly checked the condition of the drivers. The man who had caused the accident was still sitting upright in the driver's seat, looking dazed, and when she spoke to him he said in a thready voice, 'What have I done? I didn't realise…'

'Don't worry about that for the moment,' Sarah said. It seemed that his air bag had failed to deploy fully, and his leg was trapped by crumpled metal. 'Are you hurt? I've called for an ambulance. Is there anywhere in particular that's causing you pain?'

'My leg,' he said, and then added in a shaky tone, 'I'll be all right. Will you go and see to the others?'

Sarah nodded. 'I'll be back in a minute. Don't try to move.'

The driver of the other car was clutching his chest and his breathing was rapid and gasping. He was complaining of back pain, but his whole body was trembling, and Sarah guessed that he had gone into a state of shock. She stayed with him for a moment or two, trying to calm him and reassure him that he would receive medical attention soon.

It worried her that she had to leave the drivers, but her main concern had to be the young man who was lying in the road. He had been bleeding profusely from his leg wound, and she didn't know whether her attempt to stem the flow would be sufficient. She went back to him and saw that the pressure pad she had put in place was soaked with blood. The only comfort she could take was that at least he was still breathing.

It was a relief, some time later, to hear the sound of the ambulance siren in the distance, and to know that help was on its way at last. She felt out of her depth, but she knew that these people needed to be taken to hospital at the earliest opportunity. She got to her feet.

The woman who had been stopping the traffic came to stand beside her. 'The police have arrived,' she said. 'They're setting up cones to keep the area clear.'

'That's good.' The woman was much calmer now, and Sarah guessed that she would be able to give a good account to the police of what had happened.

She waited beside the motorcyclist as a paramedic walked

towards him and knelt down. He tried to talk to him, but there was no response, and so he looked up at Sarah. 'Do you know if he has been unconscious the whole time?'

'Yes, he has.' She hesitated, then added, 'The two drivers were both conscious when I went to look at them. One seems to have a chest injury and is struggling to breathe, and the other is complaining of leg pain.'

'Thanks. Perhaps you'd like to show my colleague the one with the chest pain.' He nodded towards a second paramedic who was emerging from the ambulance.

Sarah did as he'd asked, and when she was satisfied that both drivers had been assessed and the man with chest pain was being attended to she went back to the driver who had caused the pile-up and tried to reassure him that help was on the way.

By this time a second ambulance had arrived, along with a fast-response car, and more emergency practitioners began to come forward.

Feeling a trifle redundant by now, Sarah went to see how the motorcyclist was doing. The paramedic she had spoken to earlier was working side by side with someone else now, a dark-haired man who was wearing the outfit of an emergency doctor.

Sarah looked him over. Something about this man caught her attention, but she couldn't quite make up her mind what it was that was bothering her. He was kneeling down, but his demeanour was striking in that every move he made was decisive and self-assured. There was no hesitation, no doubting what needed to be done.

'As soon as I've finished intubating him, we'll splint that fractured limb,' he said. 'Once that's done we can safely transfer him to the spinal board.'

Sarah felt the hairs prickle along the back of her neck. That voice was all too familiar, and she must have inadvertently let out a breathy sigh of recognition because the man shifted his head a fraction to look up at her. He frowned.

Sarah blinked. What was Ben doing here? Was this his job, working for the emergency services? Or was he based at the local hospital? The questions were on the tip of her tongue, but she stayed silent, because right now she didn't want to distract him or in any way impede the work he was doing.

For a few seconds he held her gaze and the atmosphere seemed to be filled with tension.

'It must be something in the air,' he murmured. 'We seem fated to meet under unusual circumstances.' Then, almost as though that strange collision of minds had never happened, he simply turned away and continued attending to his patient.

It was only when the intubation was completed and the man was receiving life-giving oxygen that Ben looked at her once more and said briskly, 'If you want to do something to help, you could squeeze this oxygen bag. Keep up the momentum, and make sure you keep to a regular rhythm.'

Sarah nodded to show that she understood, and crouched down beside the young biker. 'He's still unconscious. Does he have any other injuries, apart from the leg?'

'I imagine he has a head injury, and there may be internal injuries, but we won't know until we've done scans at the hospital. Either way, it looks as though he has a broken thigh-bone, and he'll most likely need to have surgery to pin it in place. He's lost a lot of blood, but I might be able to make up for that by putting a line in and giving him fluids.' He fixed her with his dark gaze. 'What you need to do is to keep pumping the oxygen.'

Sarah did as she was told, and kept quiet so as not to distract him. The paramedic worked with him to splint the leg, and then between them they lifted him onto the protective board.

Ben stood up. 'OK, you can hand over to the paramedic now,' he told Sarah. 'I'm going to take a look at the other patients.'

'OK.' She relinquished her hold on the oxygen bag and watched Ben cautiously as he moved away, not quite understanding his abrupt manner. Perhaps he thought it strange that she had a knack of turning up in odd situations, but that was his problem, not hers.

Paramedics were getting ready to move the man who had been clutching his chest. As to the driver of the black saloon, he had been released from the driving seat and removed to a place of safety. It appeared that he was suffering from pain and swelling around his knee. To Sarah's untutored eye, it looked as though the knee had shifted in relation to his leg.

Perhaps she had said as much, because Ben glanced at her as she approached and said lightly, 'Yes, it certainly looks that way.' His mouth gave a faint twist. 'I'm surprised to find that you're still here. You're not at all squeamish, then?'

Sarah lifted her shoulders in a noncommittal shrug. She had no idea whether she was or not. As far as she was aware, this was the first time that she had come across a situation like this. 'So, what's wrong with his leg? Do you know?' she asked. 'Is there a fracture?'

'I can't be sure whether there's any fracture, but I expect the force of the smash has caused him to hit the dashboard with his leg and consequently the knee was dislocated. From the looks of the swelling and discoloration, it's quite nasty.'

He turned his attention to the patient. 'I'm afraid that your circulation is not as it should be in that limb, Colin, so I think that I should try to get the knee back in position without delay. I don't believe we can wait until we get you to the hospital.'

Colin mumbled a response, and Ben obviously took that as agreement, because he said, 'I'm going to give you something to take away the pain while I do that.' He looked directly at the man. 'As the paramedics are dealing with other patients, I'm going to ask this young woman if she will lend a hand with the procedure. Are you OK with that?'

The driver nodded, and Sarah guessed that he was in too much pain and discomfort to care one way or the other. She gave Ben a wide-eyed look.

'I've never done anything like this before,' she said in a low voice. 'Are you sure that you want me to help?'

'Quite sure.' He was already drawing up a syringe of what Sarah imagined was painkilling medication. 'All you have to do is position yourself at his head and thread your arms underneath his armpits. Clasp your hands together over his chest and keep up a counter-pressure when I pull on his leg.' He started to give the injection, glancing from time to time at his patient.

'How does that feel? Is it any easier?'

'That's better,' the man said after a while. 'The pain is going.' He gave a slow sigh, and Sarah guessed that he was feeling a surge of relief.

Ben glanced at Sarah. 'Do you think you'll be able to help me out?'

'Yes. I can do that.'

'Good. Let's get on with it, then, shall we?'

Sarah followed his instructions, kneeling down at the man's head and placing her arms around his upper torso.

Ben, in the meantime, positioned himself to grasp the man's leg in a way that would allow him to straighten it. 'Are you ready?' he asked, glancing at Sarah. 'It's really important that you counter my pulling on the limb.'

'I'm ready.'

It was all over in a matter of seconds, and as soon as Colin's leg had been straightened out, Ben started to check the circulation around the joint. 'That's improving already,' he told Colin. 'I'm going to splint it for you now, and then we'll get you into the ambulance and off to hospital.'

Sarah watched Ben as he worked. He had a sure touch, and she could see that anyone who came into his care would be well looked after. There was no hesitation, no debating what to do, and each procedure followed on from the one before like the turning of a well-oiled engine.

'Is this what you do every day?' she asked softly, as he beckoned to the paramedics who were coming from one of the ambulances.

'Emergency work, you mean?'

She nodded. 'Yes. I was wondering if you worked with the ambulance service or whether you're based at the local hospital.'

'It's a bit of both, actually.' He worked with the paramedics to lift the patient onto a stretcher, and made sure that he was strapped securely in place. 'I'm based in the A and E department at Woodvale Hospital, but I'm often called out with the ambulance service if there's a multiple accident.'

'Oh, I see.'

He studied her for a brief moment. 'What about you? Are you not at work today?'

'I was on my way to work when this happened.'

He nodded, and then directed the paramedics to transport the patient to the ambulance. 'I expect you'll be delayed for a while longer. The police will want to hear your account of what happened.'

'Yes, I imagine they will.'

He was already turning away to go with his patient, and Sarah remained where she was. Ben inclined his head briefly towards her, and then it was as though he had dismissed her from his thoughts. His attention was solely on the injured people.

That was how it should be, of course. He had been focused on his work the whole time, and finding that Sarah was already here had been just a momentary distraction, one that had actually worked to his advantage when he had enlisted her help. She doubted that he would even give her a second thought after this.

A small qualm of unease ran through her. Why did it bother her that he might so easily dismiss her from his mind? She frowned. Perhaps it was all part and parcel of her mindset since the trauma that had happened to her.

She had lost her memory and therefore she was by association unmemorable—wasn't that the case? After all, no one had come looking for her to tell her that she belonged within his or her family unit, had they? It was one more thing that made her doubt herself and wonder where she belonged.

She braced her shoulders. She had to put all that behind her. She had her child, her work and the chance of a new beginning, and wasn't it a fact that she could turn some of this to her advantage? Everything that had occurred this morning would make for an excellent news item for the local paper, wouldn't it?

It wouldn't take her long to write her exclusive account of what had gone on, and as she had her camera with her in her bag, this was an ideal opportunity for her to take some photos of the wrecked vehicles.

No sooner had the thought sparked in her mind than she started to act on it. She rapidly took several snapshots of the scene, quelling a sudden uprising of guilt by telling herself that there had been no fatalities, and that she would be foolish to miss this chance of a story. This was her livelihood after all.

Then, while she waited for the policeman to come and question her, she took out a notepad and started to draft the article.

'What do you think you're doing?'

She jumped as Ben's voice sounded in her ear. 'I'm sorry. What do you mean?'

'I saw you taking photos. How could you do that? Don't you have any sense of propriety?'

'It's my job,' she said, on a defensive note. 'I write for the local paper.'

His expression was cynical. 'Is that supposed to be an excuse? Don't we have enough people behaving like ghouls, feasting on other people's tragedies?'

'You don't know anything about the way I write,' she said, her voice taut. 'Why should you assume the worst?' She glowered at him. 'Anyway, shouldn't you be concerning yourself with your patients?'

'You're right.' He glanced over at the ambulance where the paramedic was getting ready to close the doors at the back of the vehicle. 'I can see that I'm just wasting my time talking to you.'

He walked briskly over to the ambulance and climbed in the back without a second glance in her direction.

Sarah watched the vehicle pull away, aware of a slow tide of dejection washing over her. How would he react when he discovered that she was going to be living next door to him? He had already formed the worst possible opinion of her.

She pressed her lips together. Most likely, once he was over the initial shock, he would simply leave her to her own devices.

That suited Sarah well enough. She had enough problems to cope with, without having to fathom the mindset of a reclusive neighbour.

CHAPTER THREE

'I WANT you to come into the house now, Emily,' Sarah called from the kitchen. 'I'm just getting your supper ready, and then it will be time for bed.'

Emily, though, wasn't taking too much notice of what she was saying. The overgrown garden was proving too much of a temptation, with its sheltering shrubs and lots of hidden nooks and crannies, and so far she had only managed to explore a small part of it to her satisfaction.

Moving to the cottage had been a great adventure as far as Emily was concerned, and in a way that was a relief for Sarah, because she had been worrying about what effect changing homes would have on her.

The phone rang as Sarah was about to go and bring the child into the house, and she hesitated before deciding to answer the call. Keeping an eye on the little girl through the kitchen window, Sarah picked up the receiver.

'How are you getting along?' Carol asked in a cheerful tone. 'Have you managed to make any more headway with the unpacking? I know Emily was keen to look through all the boxes.'

'I'm nearly there,' Sarah told her. 'Emily thought it was a

treasure trove, finding the toys that you had passed on to her, and I can't tell you how grateful I am to you for giving me all that bed linen and the bits and pieces for the kitchen. It was so good having you here to help out this afternoon. I don't know how I would have managed otherwise. Emily's really excited. She seems to have taken to the place, but she did make me promise that I would bring her back to see you at the weekend.'

'That would be lovely.' Sarah could feel the smile that must be on Carol's face. 'Actually, I might see you before then. I've just realised that I have a couple of good-sized rugs stored up in the attic that might come in useful for you. I had them cleaned before they went up there, so they should be in a reasonable condition, and they might make the place look a bit more cosy. I could bring them over tomorrow some time, if you like.'

'That would be great,' Sarah said.

'I'll do that, then. Perhaps I'll even get to meet your neighbour. Has there been any sign of him yet?'

Sarah winced. 'Not so far. He's been out all day. I'm not quite sure how he's going to react when he finds that we've moved in next door to him. I expect that he thought nobody would want to take the place on.'

They chatted for a while longer, until Sarah glanced out of the window and realised that she could no longer see Emily in the garden.

'I'm going to have to go and look for Emily,' she told Carol. 'She's been playing outside for the last half-hour, but it's growing dark now and I need to keep track of her in case she finds a way to get from the garden out into the fields. There's a good fence, but you know her. I wouldn't put it past her to find a way to climb over.'

'She's certainly a bundle of mischief,' Carol agreed. 'You go and find her. I'll give you a ring in the morning.'

Sarah hung up and hurried out into the garden. 'Emily, where are you?' she called.

There was no answer, and Sarah began to look around. It wasn't a particularly large garden, but the trees and shrubs cast shadows over the ground now that the light was fading, and there were so many corners that were hidden from view by trelliswork and rustic pergolas that it took several minutes of searching before she realised that Emily wasn't anywhere to be found.

A feeling of panic ran through her. She had checked the fence earlier to make sure that there weren't any gaps in it, hadn't she? Now she looked to see if Emily had used anything to help her to climb up, but there was nothing resting against the fence, except for the twisted stems and branches of climbing plants.

Alarmed now, Sarah called out again. 'Emily, I need you to tell me where you are. I'm not playing hide and seek.'

She ran her hand along the top of the fence and at one point discovered a slight indentation. It was a concealed gate, made to look as though it was part of the fence, and the bolt was on the other side. Leaning closer to get a better grip, she felt one of the panels give way slightly as her foot touched its base.

Crouching down to examine it more carefully, she realised that the wooden slats moved to one side when they were touched in a certain way, probably because some of the nails that should have held them in place from the other side were missing. Was it possible that Emily had squeezed her way through the panels and gone into the neighbouring garden?

She had to find out. Undoing the bolt, she opened the gate and went through.

Like the house it belonged to, this garden was a huge contrast to hers. It was wide, for a start, and it had been beautifully landscaped, with a velvet green lawn and low stone walls. There were curving pathways that led through ornate archways into areas beyond. Sarah followed one of the paths, peering into the shrubbery on either side.

'I don't believe this is happening,' she muttered to herself.

'Is something wrong?' The deep voice came from somewhere behind her and Sarah swung around to face her neighbour.

'Yes,' she said, recovering herself. 'There is, there definitely is, or I wouldn't be here, would I?' She flung the words at him, almost as though they were a challenge. Dismayed at being found in the wrong place at the wrong time once more, she stared at him.

'I wouldn't know about that,' Ben said. 'Going on past experience, all manner of things spring to mind.'

She gritted her teeth. Why did she have to deal with him, of all people, here and now? Wasn't it enough that she was out of her mind with worry over Emily? 'Before you start grilling me all over again, this isn't what you think.'

'I wasn't intending to do anything of the sort,' he said in a low drawl, and to her surprise, his mouth made a wry, amused shape. 'To be honest, nothing you do surprises me any more. I'm sure you'll fill me in on the details when it suits you.'

Her blue eyes glittered with frustration. 'I've lost Emily. She must have come through here, because there's nowhere else she could have gone. She wouldn't have been able to do that if you had looked after your fence properly.'

She looked around in desperation, calling out, 'Emily, I need you to come here—now.'

His dark brows lifted. 'I've no idea what you mean. The fence is fine, as far as I'm aware.'

'No, it isn't—that's just the point. The slats are loose on your side. I checked it earlier and I thought it was all right, but it isn't, and now she's gone, so I came in through the gate.' She came to a sudden halt, gathering her breath. 'And why would you need a gate in the fence anyway, if the cottage belongs to somebody else?'

'I don't think I'm following any of this.' He looked perplexed. 'Are we talking about a dog? What kind of dog is she? I suppose she must be fairly small to get through a break in the fence.'

She sent him an exasperated look. 'No…Emily's not a dog. She's my little girl. She was playing in the garden, and then she wasn't, and I don't know where she could be, except here. She's only two years old, going on three. It's not her fault. She wouldn't know that she was doing anything wrong.'

He frowned. 'I didn't realise that you had a little girl.' He shook his head. 'I dare say I should have thought of the possibility.' He glanced towards her ringless left hand and Sarah's fingers curled into a fist.

She hadn't been wearing a ring when the paramedics had found her all those months ago, but there had been a thin, pale line on her finger, which pointed to the fact that she must have worn one at one time. It was another unanswered question about her past, and one that she would rather not deal with here and now.

'I have to find her.' She waved her hands about her in an agitated gesture.

'Of course you do.' He reached out and placed the palms of his hands over her shoulders, gripping her firmly, so that she stared at him in shock. 'But first of all you need to calm down, and deal with things one at a time. How long has she been missing?'

'A few minutes.' She tried to gather her breath, but her lungs felt as though they were constricted. 'I was in the kitchen, and the phone rang, and then when I looked back she wasn't there.'

'All right, take a few deep breaths and get yourself together. We'll both look for her. She can't have gone far.' His warm hands still circled her shoulders and she realised that he wasn't going to let her go until she showed some sign that she was in control of herself.

'Yes,' she managed. 'You're probably right.' She pulled in a deep breath. 'I'm fine. You can let go of me now.'

'Are you sure?'

She nodded. 'I'm sure.'

'OK.' He slowly released her. 'Why don't you go on searching for her on this side of the garden while I go and get a torch from the house?'

Sarah hurried to do that, churned up inside because of the delay. Was Emily hiding from her, thinking that it was a game? Was that why she wasn't answering?

Ben was only gone for a minute or two, but although she had explored every part of that side of the garden while he'd been gone, she was still no nearer finding Emily.

'We'll do this area together,' he murmured, indicating the far side of the garden, 'and then, if we still haven't found her, we'll retrace our steps. I suppose she might have gone to hide behind the summerhouse.'

Some five minutes later they still hadn't found the little girl, and Sarah was beginning to feel shaky with anxiety. Ben must have sensed that because he put an arm around her, holding her in a way that was strangely comforting, considering that she barely knew him, and that for the most part they had been at loggerheads. Now, though, he was letting her know that he understood what she was going through, and that he was there for her.

'Are you quite sure that she isn't still in your garden?'

She stared at him. 'Of course I'm sure. Don't you think I've looked?' She wrenched herself free of his hold, annoyed by the suggestion.

'Even so, it wouldn't hurt to take another look, would it?' He didn't wait for her to agree with him, but walked off in the direction of the fence and went through the gate. Not knowing what else to do, Sarah followed.

'It isn't as though it's that big a garden,' she said. 'I've checked everywhere.'

'Hmm.' He was looking around. 'Did you think to look in the shed?'

'Yes,' she said crossly, 'I did, even though I don't believe she could manage the door.'

'What about the dog kennel?'

'Dog kennel?' She frowned. 'I told you, I don't have a dog.'

'Maybe not, but there is a kennel. Haven't you seen it?'

She shook her head, looking baffled. 'Where would that be?'

'The last time I saw it, it was underneath the old tarpaulin at the back of the shed. I don't suppose you would have clambered over all the rubbish at the back there, because you would assume that there was no space for anything beneath all that junk.'

'I did look over there, but all I could see was old chairs and pieces of wood and general clutter.'

'Well, let's take a look now.' He handed her the torch. 'Shine that in the general direction of the back of the shed while I move a few things. It's quite possible that a small child could have squeezed through the gap to get to the kennel.'

'I didn't know that the old gentleman who lived here had a dog,' she murmured.

'He did for a time.'

While he was talking, he was busy moving junk out of the way, and Sarah was amazed to see a large wooden kennel gradually appear. The opening to the kennel was slightly hidden from her view, and now she moved forward to take a look inside.

'Oh, thank heaven,' she said on a breathy sigh of relief. 'She's here… She must have been here all the time.' She turned round to face him, a smile widening her mouth. 'She's fast asleep, curled up in the corner.' She reached out and touched his arms, squeezing him gently, full of the joy of finding her little girl. 'Thank you so much… I just would never have thought that she would be here.'

If he was startled by her enthusiastic reaction, he recovered soon enough, and stepped back so that she could crouch down and lift out the sleeping child. A moment later she straightened up, the little girl nestled safely in her arms. Sarah bent her head and gently kissed her cheek.

'I'll take her back into the house.' She glanced up at him. 'Would you like to come in with me, and I'll put the kettle on?' The euphoria of finding Emily meant that the words were out of her mouth before she had time to reconsider, but within moments she was feeling a chill of caution.

The last time she had seen him, he had accused her of ghoulish behaviour because of her work for the newspaper, and his opinion of her must be really low.

Regardless of that, he had helped her to look for Emily, but how long would it be before it dawned on him that she and her daughter had moved in for good and that his splendid isolation was gone for the foreseeable future?

That was something that worked both ways, wasn't it? But, whatever their differences, the invitation had already been uttered.

'That would be good, thanks. It seems like hours since I've had anything to drink, and I'm feeling quite parched.'

He pushed open the back door for her so that she could go through with her precious bundle. Once in the brightly lit kitchen, Emily began to stir.

'Did I been sleep?'

'Yes, sunbeam, you have.'

Emily stretched and stared about her, and when she saw Ben, her eyes grew large. 'Who is you?' she said.

He smiled. 'I'm Ben. I live next door.'

'In the big house?'

He nodded. 'That's right.'

'I found a little house,' she told him. 'It was as big as this.' She spread her arms wide to show the extent of it.

'I know you did. That's where we found you. You were lying in the dog kennel, fast asleep.'

'It's the doggie's house?' Emily was astonished by that piece of information.

He nodded. 'It was, but not any more. I think you'll be able to play in it from now on.'

Emily beamed a smile at him. 'Where's the doggy?'

'He's not here any more.'

She seemed content with that, and when Sarah set her gently down on the floor, she hurried away to find her toys. 'I go play,' she said.

'Yes, but not for long,' Sarah warned. 'You need to have your supper and get ready for bed.'

She glanced at Ben. 'Sit yourself down,' she said, pointing to a chair by the table, before busying herself with the kettle. 'How did you know that the kennel was there, behind the shed?'

'I've always known about it. The house I'm living in was my parents' home originally, and the kennel belonged to our Labrador. That was a long time ago, though, and my mother suggested that I pass it on to Alfred for his dog.'

'Your mother?' She stopped what she was doing and stared at him.

He gave a wry smile. 'I do have one, you know. Don't we all?'

Her expression wavered, and he looked at her curiously. 'I... Yes, of course,' she murmured. A familiar tide of help-lessness washed over her. What did she know about her par-entage? To cover her unease, she filled the kettle with water at the sink and then flicked the switch. 'What happened to your mother? Do you mind me asking?'

He shook his head. 'Some time after my father died, my mother realised that she wanted to live in a house that was smaller and more manageable, so she moved to the nearby village. I've always liked this area, so I bought the house from her.'

'That sounds like a sensible idea all round.' She studied him as he eased his back against the sturdy wooden chair and thrust his long legs out before him. He was wearing casual clothes, black trousers and a cotton shirt that was open at the collar. He looked faintly weary, and she remembered that he'd said it had been a long while since he'd had anything to drink. Perhaps he hadn't eaten either.

'Would you like to have some supper with us?' she asked. 'It won't be much, because I don't have a cooker that works as yet. I made a salad, though, and there are crusty bread rolls, and I was going to heat up some soup in the microwave. I just need to unpack the soup bowls from the box.'

'Thanks. I'd appreciate that. I've been out with the cave rescue team all day, and I'd only just arrived home when you appeared in the garden.'

'Cave rescue?' Sarah started to ask him about that when Emily decided to join the conversation.

'Mummy forgetted to bring the plates and knives and forks,' she told Ben earnestly, 'so we couldn't eat our lunch. We had to go and get fish and chips from the village for our lunch.'

'Did you?' He widened his eyes. 'Well, you know, fish and chips are good.'

Emily nodded. 'I like them.'

Ben glanced around the kitchen. 'It looks as though you have some plates and cutlery now.'

'Auntie Carol bringed them.'

'Oh, I see.' He looked at Sarah. 'You have a sister who lives nearby?'

She could almost feel him thinking, *There are two of you?* 'Actually, no,' she murmured. Seeing his confusion, she added drily, 'It's a long story.'

'Ah.' He inclined his head to one side. 'I should have

known. You seem to live quite a complicated life, one way and another.' He made to stand up. 'Shall I give you a hand with the meal?'

'No, that's all right. It will only take me a minute or two to get things ready. Sit tight.' She glanced at him. 'You mentioned cave rescue. What's that all about?'

'It's something I do. I'm on the roster with the cave rescue team, so I tend to be called out every so often. I've been down near Castleton today. There was a report that some youths were late coming back from a trip down one of the caves. Their parents called it in because they were worried that they might have been hurt.'

Sarah could imagine how concerned the parents must have been. 'Did you manage to find them?' She covered the wooden table with a cloth and began to lay out a bowl of salad, along with quiche and grated cheese.

'We did. The entrance to the cave is low and wide, but the pathway narrows as you go along and there are several passages leading from the main one. I think the boys were intent on looking at the fossils down there. A section of the river trickles down through the limestone and widens out at one point, so there was always the worry that they had got themselves into difficulty.'

'Had they?'

'Yes, but not because of the water—well, indirectly, they did. As the water passes through the rock, there is sometimes a freeze-thaw effect that tends to widen the crevices as time goes on. That seems to have happened in this instance because there was a collapse of rocks in the tunnel and they were blocked in.'

Sarah was faintly horrified to hear this. 'Those poor boys

must have been terrified. Did you manage to get them out? Were they hurt?'

He nodded. 'Yes, we brought them out, eventually. There were five of them altogether. They had cuts and bruises, and all of them were very cold, but one young lad was suffering from hypothermia. He had fallen into the water, and the cold had affected him so much that his heart rate was slow and weak and he appeared to be slipping into unconsciousness.'

Sarah frowned. 'So, if you'd reached him later, things could have been much worse? What did you do? Were you able to bring him round?' She called to Emily to come and have her hands washed, but she scarcely took her eyes off Ben, anxious to hear the outcome.

'We did eventually. We took off his wet outer garments and covered him with special insulating blankets and then lifted him out to the ambulance. As soon as we were able to, we gave him oxygen that had been heated a little, and gradually he started to come round. All of the boys are fine now.'

Sarah lifted Emily up and sat her on the worktop, washing her hands with a flannel. 'I'm glad to hear it,' she said. Settling Emily down on a chair, she handed her a mug of soup. 'I've cooled it down for you, but you should drink it slowly,' she told the child.

Turning to Ben, she said, 'Help yourself to food. I'll pour the tea for you, and you can help yourself to milk and sugar.'

Sitting down opposite him a minute or two later, she said, 'Do you know what happened to the people we saw in the accident the other day? I rang the hospital, but they wouldn't tell me very much.'

He smiled teasingly. 'I expect they were wary of reporters.'

She sent him a quick glance. 'There was nothing wrong

with my article. If anything, it might serve as a warning to other people not to overtake on a bend or the brow of a hill.'

'Yes, I read your piece. I must say, it was very well written, and you were very careful not to lay the blame anywhere, but just quoted what other people had said.' He tasted the soup, and remarked softly, 'This is good.'

'I'm glad you like it. Not that I had anything to do with making it—I don't really have the facilities as yet.' She continued to look at him, waiting to see if he would enlighten her on the condition of the patients.

He broke a corner off one of the crusty rolls and bit into it before going on. 'As to the injured people, they are all doing reasonably well. The driver whose car was hit had a broken rib but was otherwise fine, and the driver of the black car was kept under observation for a while before being sent home. His knee will be in a splint for quite a while.' He paused to take another bite of the bread.

'And the motorcyclist? I know that he was badly injured.' Sarah helped Emily with her bread, and the little girl gave both of them a smile, with greasy smudges either side of her mouth from the butter and an upper lip that was outlined with soup.

'Yes, he was. He had a head injury, but he regained consciousness in hospital, and then he went for surgery on the leg. They expect that he will make a full recovery.'

'That's good to hear.'

He nodded. 'It was probably because of you that he survived. At the hospital the driver of the car that hit him told me that he saw you take off your jacket and use it to stem the bleeding.'

'I just did what I felt was right.'

'You did well.' He studied her. 'So, how long have you been working for the local paper?'

'Just a couple of months. I started by doing the occasional article, mostly about events around the town and villages, but then I discovered that I had a knack for writing medical features. I've been sending them more and more pieces lately, and a few weeks ago they gave me a weekly column. It isn't much, but it's enough to keep the wolf from the door.'

Ben speared grated cheese with his fork. 'That must have been a happy event for you. What did you do before the news-paper work?'

Sarah didn't answer right away. Instead, she busied herself wiping Emily's face, and then she quietly told the little girl that she could get down from the table. 'I want you to go and get ready for bed,' she murmured. 'I'll come up and help you in a little while. See if you can manage your pyjamas by yourself.'

Emily was happy to oblige, and skipped off to climb the stairs.

Sarah turned her attention back to Ben and pulled in a slow breath. They were going to be neighbours, and sooner or later he would begin to wonder about certain aspects of her life.

'The truth is,' she told him, 'I don't know what I did before journalism. I was taken to hospital after a head injury, and I have no knowledge of what went before.'

He frowned, not taking his gaze off her. 'Do you know how you came to have a head injury?'

'I only know what they told me at the hospital. Apparently, I was with Emily, and it looks as though we were on a journey together. I had stopped off at a shop to buy a snack, and I asked the shopkeeper about hotels in the area. I said that we weren't going to be able to reach our destination before nightfall, and I had decided that we would stop somewhere overnight.'

She hesitated, taking a moment to sip her drink and allow time for her feelings of agitation to subside. Ben remained quiet, waiting patiently for her to go on.

'I went outside the shop, and I must have decided to use a phone box to call one of the hotels, but I didn't get as far as doing that. It looks as though someone must have tried to snatch my bag and my car keys, and apparently I put up a fight, because I was knocked to the ground and I hit my head on a wall as I fell. Whoever did that to me made off with my car and all my belongings.'

'So you had no identity on you, nothing that would give any clue as to who you were or where you were going?'

Sarah shook her head. 'There was nothing. There wasn't even any CCTV footage to show the car that I was driving. The only thing they knew was that I had a child, because Emily stayed with me, and when the paramedics came she said, 'Mummy hurt...bad man hurt Mummy.'

She winced at the scene she pictured in her mind of Emily waiting beside her, alone and frightened.

'Did they never find the car or the man?'

'No, they didn't.' She grimaced. 'I don't suppose they ever will now.'

He stared at her. 'It must have been a bad head injury, if you remember nothing. Do you remember anything at all?'

'It was bad enough that I was in hospital for a few weeks. As to remembering anything, I have images in my mind sometimes, but they come and go before I can latch onto them. I told the doctors and the police that my name was

Sarah Hall, because that was the first thing that came into my mind. Emily seemed to know her name and that ought to have confirmed it, but they haven't found any records to show that's who I am.' She gave a rueful smile. 'Emily said my name was Sarah, so I guess that must be right, at least.'

Ben finished eating and carefully pushed his plate to one side. 'What happened to Emily while you were in hospital?'

'Social Services found a foster-family for her—Carol and Tom. They have been very good to both of us. Emily was traumatised by what had happened, so much so that she could barely speak about it, apparently, and Carol did everything she could to help her through that difficult time. Then, when I came out of hospital, they helped me to get back on my feet.' She pulled in a shaky breath. 'I stayed with them for several months, but I began to feel that I had to find my own way. That's why I made the decision to come and live here, even though Carol thought it wasn't a good idea. She was worried that I wasn't ready.'

'I think I agree with Carol. A head injury that causes you to lose your memory to such an extent is very serious. You need somebody with you while you learn about who you are and how to cope with everyday life. I expect you must have all sorts of problems on a day-to-day basis.'

Sarah stood up and began to clear away the crockery. 'I'm all right,' she said. 'I'll get by.'

His gaze flicked over her. 'It's not enough to get by, though, is it? Especially when you have a small child with you. And it's certainly too much of a responsibility for you to be taking on a property like this one.' He came to his feet.

'I don't think so,' she told him. 'I made the decision, and I'm going to stick by it. I have to start somewhere to make a life of our own.' She sent him a cool, assessing look. He was going to be a thorn in her side, she could feel it as surely as he was standing there, facing her.

'I'll help you with the dishes,' he said, but she shook her head.

'No… Thank you, but…no. I have to go upstairs and put Emily to bed. I'm sure you have other things that you should be doing, so I'll say goodnight to you. Thank you for helping me to find Emily.'

He looked at her as though he was going to give her an argument, but after a moment or two he must have decided otherwise because he inclined his head briefly and said, 'Goodnight, then, and thank you for the supper. I'll leave you to yourself.'

She watched him go, her mind sparking with all kinds of doubts and uncertainties. He was like all the rest, believing that she would make a mess of things. What would it take for her to prove everyone wrong?

CHAPTER FOUR

RAIN was falling steadily outside, a dreary, relentless downpour that swamped everything in its path, and more than matched Sarah's mood.

She frowned as she looked about the kitchen. Where on earth would be the best place for her to start? Taking on this cottage had seemed like a good idea at the time, but that had been before she had actually moved in and realised the full extent of what needed to be done.

This morning, as she prepared to take Emily to nursery, she had decided it was the ideal opportunity for her to make some headway with putting the place to rights. Of course, she hadn't been expecting the health visitor to drop by and since then her plans had changed. The health visitor had been there to look into the welfare of children under five in the area, and hadn't realised that Emily would be at the nursery that morning.

Now Sarah's priorities were all mixed up, and she was torn between continuing to scrub the Aga or whether she should be stripping the wallpaper from Emily's room, ready for decorating. It was bad enough that Carol, her child's foster-mother, and Ben, her neighbour, believed she wouldn't be able to cope, without having the doubts of the health visitor ringing in her ears.

A knock at the kitchen door brought her sharply out of her introspection. What now? Was this someone else ready to write her off as incapable?

Heaving a sigh, she went to open the door and found Ben standing there. For a moment she simply frowned. She hadn't seen much of him these last few days, and she had wondered if he had been staying away deliberately. No matter. That suited her well enough.

'Is it that bad?' he said, giving her a narrowed look from under his dark lashes. 'Only I saw that your car was outside and I guessed you were back from dropping Emily off.'

So he knew where she had been. Was he keeping an eye on her from a distance and contenting himself with watching her every move? Or maybe she was becoming paranoid and under the illusion that the whole world was conspiring against her. Perhaps that was yet another symptom of the aftermath of a head injury.

She pulled the door open wider and waved a hand towards the kitchen. 'Would you like to come in? I was just about to make some coffee, if you'd like some.' The last thing she needed right now was a visitor, but it would have been churlish to send him away.

'Thanks.' He stepped inside the room and she closed the door behind him.

'Everything's a mess,' she said. 'I started to try to clean up the old range cooker but there was an interruption and now I haven't the heart to go on with it.'

He glanced around. 'Actually, you've made a good job of it so far. I didn't imagine it would come up looking anywhere near as good as it does.' He went to take a closer look. 'It hasn't been used in years because the burners were blocked and Alfred didn't do much proper cooking, but from the look of things you've managed to sort them out.'

'Well, hopefully I have, but I'm not quite ready to put it to the test.' She set about making coffee for both of them and then sent him a cautious look. 'Was there something you particularly wanted to see me about, or are you just being neighbourly?'

His mouth quirked. 'A bit of both. I've been having a clear-out, and I just thought you might find some use for these curtains I found in the airing cupboard. They look to me like good quality but, of course, you might not agree. I could always throw them out.'

Sarah inspected the bundle he produced. The curtains were made of fine linen, and were softly patterned in a pale rose that would look beautiful in the living room.

'You shouldn't throw them out,' she said. 'That would be a total waste. They're lovely…but as to me using them, I don't know what to say. According to the health visitor, this place isn't particularly suitable for Emily, with the damp and the cold bedrooms, and now I'm so on edge about everything that I don't know what to do. I feel as though I ought to leave, but I've just signed a six-month lease.'

He frowned. 'Has she said that you shouldn't stay here?'

'No. It was just an opinion she gave me, and she seemed to agree that it could probably all be put right within a few weeks.'

'Well, that's true enough. It's only damp in the kitchen, and that could be attended to.'

'Yes, but the landlord, Alfred's son, isn't prepared to act on it, and I can't afford to deal with it.'

She straightened, sucking air into her lungs, and made an effort to get a grip on herself. Hadn't he told her that she wouldn't be able to cope just a few days ago? Wasn't she just playing straight into his hands? 'You caught me at a bad time,' she murmured. 'Forget what I said. Of course I'll sort it out. I'll get a couple of heaters in and see if that will solve the problem.'

'Actually, I don't think it will,' he said. 'I think the trouble stems from an inadequate damp course in one part of the outer wall. It needs expert treatment.'

Sarah's chin lifted. 'Then I'll just have to get someone in, and hope that I can sell a few freelance articles elsewhere.'

He shook his head. 'I don't think that will be necessary. I'll have a word with the landlord as I know the family, and make sure that something is done about it. In the meantime, I'll send someone round to take a look at the situation.'

Sarah stared at him. Did nothing ever faze him? He seemed to have an answer for everything.

'That's very good of you—but I don't want you to feel that you have to help me out. I may look helpless, but I'm not.'

He gave a wry smile. 'I think I'm beginning to realise that,' he said. 'You certainly took things into your own hands when you found that the estate agent had given you the wrong key, and as to the accident the other day, I thought you did a great job of dealing with the injured.'

Her spirits lifted a little at his words. So he didn't think that she was a hopeless case after all?

He began to wander about the kitchen, and her gaze followed him, absorbing the lithe movements of his body, the relaxed swing of his arms, the long legs encased in dark trousers. He stopped by the wooden table, his hand absently touching the typescript of the article she was preparing to hand over to her editor. The papers shifted, and as he put them neatly back in place his glance must have skimmed over some of what she had written. It was an article about vaccinations for people who were about to go on holiday.

'How is it that you know so much about medical things?' he asked.

'I don't know,' she said. 'It just seems to come naturally— although I have to do my research, of course.' She paused. 'I did go on a first-aid course two or three months ago. I thought it would be a kind of therapy for me.'

He nodded. 'That was probably a wise move. It's always handy to know what to do in an emergency.'

She pushed a mug towards him. 'Be careful, the coffee's hot.' She realised as soon as she'd said it that he didn't need to be told what to do. The fact was, she was used to telling Emily to take care, and it was an automatic observation.

He made no comment, but accepted the coffee and sipped gratefully. 'How would you feel about taking on extra work?' he asked, looking at her over the rim of the cup. 'Would you want to do that, or would it be a problem because of your need to look after Emily?'

'I'd like to be able to earn enough to do more than just survive,' she said. Her blue eyes were troubled, and she ran a hand distractedly through her honey curls. His gaze lifted to follow the action.

Feeling a little self-conscious under that scrutiny, she added, 'I'm sure that Carol would be only too glad to help out where Emily is concerned, but I'm really not skilled at anything in particular, as far as I know, and the writing doesn't bring in much of an income at the moment. I don't know of anyone who would want to take me on right now.'

'I could think of somewhere that you might fit in perfectly,' he murmured.

She lifted a brow. 'Where would that be?'

'With the ambulance service.' He took another swallow of his coffee. 'I know that the admin people at the health authority where I work are looking for someone to work with the paramedics—not in any kind of medical capacity but to follow them for a period of time and write a report on their day-to-day activities. It's part of a regional initiative to see whether any changes might be made to improve the way we do things.'

Sarah frowned. 'Surely the paramedics would object to that? I certainly wouldn't want someone following me around, noting down everything that I do.'

He shook his head. 'You wouldn't be checking up on them. It's more that you would keep a record of things such as how many casualties they have to deal with at any one time, the difficulties they have in getting to the patients, how the equipment is used, the way medication is given to patients, and then, when all the information has been gathered, experts can evaluate what might be done to improve the system. Maybe they would suggest extra equipment be provided if it would help to make the job easier.'

'So it's a kind of survey, taken over several weeks, that might help them to plan future operations?'

He nodded. 'In a nutshell, yes, that's about it. I think you'd be ideal for that. You wouldn't have to work full time, and you could probably fit it in around Emily being at nursery.' His gaze skimmed over her. 'What do you think?'

'I think I need time to mull it over. Do I have to give my answer right away?'

'No, of course not. But don't leave it too long, because I know they want to take someone on fairly soon, and I could put a word in for you. You would have to go through an interview, but I can't see that there would be any problems.'

Sarah had to acknowledge that it would certainly make her life a lot easier if it worked out all right. 'OK, I'll give it some thought, and maybe have a word with Carol. I could let you know tomorrow, if that's all right?'

'That'll be fine.' He glanced down at the watch on his wrist. 'I should go—I have to be at work in half an hour. I'll see you later on. Thanks for the coffee.'

After he had gone, Sarah looked about her. Why was it that things seemed so different now, so desolate without his presence in her big, empty kitchen? Her moods seemed to swing from one extreme to another these days. But wasn't that the whole point of her moving in here? She was an adult, and she had to learn to manage by herself, to cope with everything that life threw at her.

At all costs, she would have to avoid getting used to having Ben around. He was going out of his way to help, but it wouldn't do to rely on him because she knew, more than anyone, how the rug could be pulled out from under your feet and a person's whole, cosy existence could be annihilated in one swoop of fate.

She turned her attention back to the cooker, and set about cleaning it with renewed vigour. The action helped to rid her of some of her frustrations.

It was around a fortnight later that Sarah was due to start work with the ambulance service. She had been asked to report to the ambulance station next to the hospital to meet the man who would be acting as her manager initially, but Ben fore-stalled her by turning up at her front door with the fast-response car.

'I'll take you into work, and drop you off back here,' he told her. 'You'll be riding with me.'

She frowned. 'I don't think I follow,' she said. 'I'd assumed that I would be going with the paramedics in the ambulance.'

'You'll do that, eventually,' he said, holding open the car door for her and indicating that she should slide into the passenger seat, 'but I'll be working with you for the first few weeks to show you the ropes and help ease you into the job.'

She narrowed her eyes, watching him as he climbed into the driver's seat and started the engine. This wasn't at all what she had been expecting. Had he engineered this whole thing? Was this just another way of keeping an eye on her? Why was everyone so certain that she wouldn't be able to manage her own affairs? How could she ever be independent if no one was going to leave her to work things out for herself?

'Did you plan all this?' she enquired once they were on their way, heading towards their first call. Her tone was edged with a hint of steel, and if he noticed her annoyance, he wasn't letting on.

'I don't know what you mean,' he said, throwing her a sidelong glance. 'It was suggested that I liaise with you initially. I'm simply following instructions.'

She would believe that in a month of Sundays. Why hadn't he mentioned it before now? Her eyes glittered as she watched him drive. If the suggestion had been made, it had most likely come from him in the first place. He was totally in control, supremely confident in everything that he did.

'I thought you were supposed to be based in A and E?'

'I am usually, but we have a rota system in place so I'll be with the ambulance team for a month, and then another doctor will take over. Anyway, it'll help you to have someone medically trained to guide you through the initial stages.'

She could hardly argue with that, but it seemed to her that everything that was happening had his imprint on it.

'Where are we going?' she asked in a taut voice. 'You do realise, I hope, that I'm not just along for the ride? I have a job to do, so some input would come in handy.'

'Of course it would,' he said smoothly. 'We're heading to the outskirts of town, some ten miles from here. A bus was in collision with a car, and it looks as though there are a number of casualties. We'll have back-up from police and fire crews.'

'Has there been a fire?'

'No, but they'll use cutting equipment to free people if necessary.' He glanced at her. 'Are you OK with that?'

'I'm fine,' she said, already busying herself with making notes.

When she had finished with that, she was content to sit back and watch the scenery go by. Ben wasn't making conversation, and she was glad of that, because anything she had to say to him would probably come out wrong just now. It wouldn't surprise her at all to discover that he had told Admin exactly how her job needed to be set out.

The landscape, at least, was soothing to her battered nerves. They were passing through a green valley, where the river cut its way through beds of millstone grit and shale, and graceful trees of silver birch, larch and beech marked its course. In the far distance she could see a gorge, carved out of the limestone, where water tumbled over rocks and birds flitted across the blue sky to nest in sheltered crags.

'We should be there in another minute or so,' Ben said at last. 'You might want to take a note of the type of equipment that the paramedics use, and see if they have any particular difficulties with any of the procedures.'

'I imagine any problems they have would be centred on the number of casualties,' she remarked in a stiff voice.

'Yes, that too.'

When she climbed out of the car a short time later, the first thing she noted was that the bus was slightly tipped on its side, prevented from toppling over completely by a sturdy tree on a bend in the road. Without the tree the damage would probably have been much worse but, as far as she could see, there was shattered glass around, and she hoped fervently that no one had been seriously hurt by it.

Sarah went to see if she could help in any way, and was directed by the man in charge to where the paramedics were tending to people with cuts and bruises. She helped to give oxygen to a girl who was in shock, while Matt went to tend to the driver of the car, who was trapped by the metalwork of the door.

They could definitely do with more people on hand to deal with patients, she noted, but the paramedics coped brilliantly, reassuring the wounded and despatching them to the ambulances with care and efficiency.

When the girl she was tending was transferred to the waiting vehicle, Sarah went to see what Ben was doing. She found him treating one of the bus passengers, a man who was lying by the roadside. He didn't appear to be breathing, and Ben was giving him chest compressions.

'Is there anything I can do?' she asked.

He nodded. 'Take over here with the compressions while

I get the defibrillator ready. I suspect he's having a heart attack and I need to bring his heart rhythm back to normal.'

He showed her where to place her hands, and she continued with the compressions while he set up the machine.

'OK, I'm going to place the electrode pads on his chest.' He worked quickly, and then said, 'Stand clear.'

Sarah did as she was told, and was immediately impressed by the automated action of the machine. It appeared to analyse the patient's rhythm as ventricular fibrillation, and then delivered a shock that was designed to send the heart back into a normal rhythm. After a couple of shocks had been administered, the man suddenly made a gasping sound, and Sarah could see from the monitor that his heart rhythm had changed.

Having asked his name, Ben set about reassuring his patient as the man started to come round. 'I'm going to give you oxygen, Steven, to help you with your breathing.' While he put the mask in place, he asked, 'Do you remember anything of what happened to you?'

'There was an accident,' Steven said hesitantly. 'A car came out of nowhere and cut across the bus.' He paused to suck air into his lungs. 'We took the corner too wide, and I felt the bus start to tip over.' Sarah noticed that he was beginning to shake a little, but after a moment he went on, 'I thought I was done for.'

'You're going to be all right,' Ben told him. 'You had a bit of a scare and it sent your heart into an abnormal rhythm, but things are looking much better now. We're going to put you in the ambulance and take you to hospital so that you can be checked out properly.'

'OK…thanks.'

After he had made sure that Steven was settled comfortably in the vehicle, Ben left him with the paramedics and came back to Sarah.

'You might want to make a note of the patient's response to the defibrillator,' he suggested. 'We'll do a follow-up to show how he progressed after treatment at the hospital, and then again in several months' time.'

'I've already done that,' she said. 'They told me about the survey at the interview. One of the biggest parts of the job is noting down how the defibrillator is used and the results it produces.' Perhaps he had thought she might not be focused, but she would show him that she was on board with everything.

'That's great.' He gave her a swift grin. 'You should try to relax a bit. I'm not on your case. I'm actually on your side and, in fact, this job could have gone to anyone of a number of people, but I'm glad that you were the one who landed it.'

She absorbed that snippet of information with a faint sense of resignation. Perhaps it was true that she had been a fraction uptight that morning. He had helped her out by suggesting that she apply for the job, and he had done everything to smooth her path, and not made one comment about her truculent attitude. She was an ungrateful wretch.

The rest of the day passed in a relatively smooth manner, or maybe it was just that Ben made it seem that way. Whatever type of callout they had to attend, he did his job in a skilled, efficient way, and his manner with his patients was unfailingly kind and reassuring.

By the end of the afternoon, Sarah felt a growing respect for him. 'You seem like someone who enjoys his work,' she commented when they were on their way home. 'Perhaps "enjoy" is the wrong word, given what you have to deal with, but you never seem to put a foot wrong.'

He sent her an oblique glance before giving his attention to the road ahead once more. 'I have to say that you've surprised me, too. You don't seem at all fazed by the situations we've come across. Some people just wouldn't be able to cope.'

She smiled. 'That's one advantage I have, then. I've no idea where it came from, but it has to be good, doesn't it?'

'That's true enough.' He turned the car onto the country lane leading to the village where Sarah had lived for a while with Carol and Tom. 'Would you mind if I looked in on my mother before we go back to the hospital?' he asked. 'She hasn't been feeling well of late, and I want to find out how she got on when the doctor called today. We could stop by and pick up Emily first, if you like, and then I could drop you off at home later. There's no need for you to go back to the hospital.'

Sarah nodded. 'That's fine by me.' She sent him a quick glance. 'Has someone being looking after your mother? It must be a worry for you if she lives on her own.'

'I made sure that someone would be with her off and on throughout the last couple of weeks. She ought to have been in hospital really but, being stubborn as usual, she wouldn't agree to it.'

Sarah frowned. 'I'm sorry. What's wrong with her, if you don't mind me asking?'

'She had flu earlier in the year, and it left her feeling really groggy for a while. Then she developed pleurisy. She's been finding it difficult to breathe easily, and she gets tired very quickly. I keep telling her that she has to rest, but she insists on trying to do things.'

'That must be difficult for you. I think I would worry if

something happened to Carol or Tom, and I've only known them for a few months.' It troubled her greatly that she couldn't remember her own parents, and it seemed as though Carol and Tom had taken their place.

Emily was in a joyful mood when Sarah stopped to collect her from Carol's house. 'We been to park,' she said. 'I played on the swings, and we threw bread for the ducks. They was so greedy.' She opened her eyes wide, recalling the day's events.

'It sounds as though you've had a lovely time,' Sarah said, giving her a hug before thanking Carol for collecting her from nursery. She introduced Carol to Ben, and the two of them seemed to hit it off right away.

'I hear that you're sorting out the damp problem for Sarah,' Carol said. 'She told me that the men came along to inject the damp course with sealant, and it looks as though it's doing the trick. I only hope that the landlord is going to reimburse you for the work.'

'He will,' Ben said. 'We managed to hammer out an agreement between us.'

Sarah wondered what kind of agreement that would have been, but as she was about to delve deeper, Carol asked, 'So how did the new job go?'

'It was all right,' Sarah said. 'As it turned out, Ben was working with me, so if there was anything I didn't understand I just had to ask. I think I'm getting the hang of everything.'

'She's doing fine,' Ben said.

'That's good to hear.' Carol glanced at Sarah once more. 'It will perk you up to get out and about,' she said. 'Perhaps you were right, after all, about needing to get back into the outside world—all this going out and about might help to prod your memory into coming back.'

'Let's hope so.'

They chatted for a little while longer then went out to Ben's car. Carol produced a child's seat from the garage loft and, once Emily was safely strapped in, they set off once more.

Ben's mother lived just a short distance away, on the far side of the village. Her house was stone built, with a low sloping roof and rambling clematis growing around the front door. There were window-boxes beneath each casement window, blooming with brightly coloured nemesia and a pretty assortment of surfinias.

She answered the door to them, and Sarah could see straight away that she was an open and friendly woman. She was much more frail than Sarah had expected, with a slender frame and chestnut hair that was fading to grey around the temples. Her eyes were the same deep grey as Ben's, though, and she clearly adored her son.

'I told you that you didn't need to visit every day,' she said, greeting him with a kiss, and ushering them all into the house. 'It's lovely to see you, but I know how busy you are.'

She turned to look at Sarah and Emily, giving them both a smile. Her gaze shifted down to Emily, her eyes widening. 'And who are these people, I wonder? Here's a beautiful little girl, and from that lovely blonde hair that you both have, I imagine that you must be mother and daughter. Am I right?'

Emily nodded vigorously. 'My mummy been to work.' She frowned. 'I don't go work…I go nursery. I been nursery today, and we maked gingerbread men.' She waved a plastic box in the air. 'Do you want one?'

'Oh, I think that would be lovely. Yes, please. Do you know, they are my favourite things to eat? Ben's, too, next to flapjacks.'

Emily's smile was as wide as could be and she eagerly followed Ben's mother as she led the way along the hall.

'If we're to have gingerbread men,' the woman told Emily, 'I'd better put the kettle on. We'll have a cup of tea.'

Sarah noticed that her breathing was laboured, and Ben must have seen it, too, because he said, 'You should go and sit yourself down. I'll make the tea, and then you can tell me what the GP had to say.'

'You worry too much. I'm fine. He told me to keep taking the tablets and get plenty of rest.' She showed them into a light, comfortably furnished room that had French doors to one side, opening out onto a small garden.

'I hope you don't mind us dropping in on you this way,' Sarah said. 'Ben was keen to make sure that you were all right. He said you've been quite ill lately.'

'I think I'm over the worst,' his mother said. 'They gave me antibiotics, and I have tablets to take away the pain when I breathe.' She paused to drag air into her lungs. 'My neighbours have been really good to me, and Ben has dropped by every day to make sure that I was resting. I feel bad about that, because I know he has such a difficult job to do.'

'I think you're more important to him than his job,' Sarah commented. 'He was concerned that you weren't being treated in hospital.'

'I wouldn't have liked that.'

She would have said more, but Emily suddenly blurted out, 'What's your name?'

'I'm Jennifer,' Ben's mother told her. 'And you must be Emily.'

'How do you know that?' Emily stared at her, open-mouthed. 'How do you know my name?'

Jennifer sat down in a chintz-covered armchair and pointed out a matching settee to Sarah. 'Well, you see…Ben told me all about you and your mother. He said that you'd come to live next door to him. I've been looking forward to meeting you.'

Ben came into the room and began to set down a tray of cups and saucers on a table by the far wall. 'I brought biscuits and cakes, just in case there aren't enough gingerbread men to go round.'

Emily sat down on the settee beside Sarah and began to swing her legs to and fro. She was gazing intently at Jennifer, watching her every movement. 'I thought you was my nana,' she told the older woman. 'I haven't seed my nana and grandad for—' she spread her arms wide '—ages and ages.'

'Oh, dear, haven't you? That's a shame. Perhaps they've gone away somewhere.'

Sarah's jaw dropped as soon as she heard Emily's words, and she drew a painful intake of breath as her throat constricted with warring emotions. As far as she could recall, this was the first time that the child had mentioned any grandparents. It was like receiving a blow to her stomach, and for a moment or two she bent forward a little, trying to hide her reaction.

Emily nodded, obviously mulling over the idea that the grandparents might have gone away, and before she had time to ask any more questions, Jennifer said in a thoughtful voice, 'Do you know, I think I have some little dollies in my workbox. I was making them for a craft fair, but you could play with them if you like.'

'Yes, please,' Emily answered, her tone eager.

'I'll get them,' Ben said. Sarah felt his glance run over her, and there was a hint of concern in his eyes. A moment or two later Jennifer came and sat down beside her, laying a hand gently on her arm. 'Are you all right?'

'Yes.' Sarah straightened up. 'It was nothing. I don't know what I was thinking. It was just a bit of a shock hearing her talk about her nana and grandad. I didn't even know that she called them by those names. She hardly ever talks about the past, and I'm not sure whether that's because she doesn't remember or because she can't express what she's feeling.' She could see that Emily was happily playing across the room, investigating the lovely outfits that Jennifer had made for the dolls.

'Ben told me that you had lost your memory,' Jennifer said softly. 'Have you never talked to Emily about her grandparents?'

Sarah shook her head. 'I was afraid that it would upset her. She was in such a state after seeing what happened to me, and we all had to be so careful in what we said to her for fear of making her more stressed. She never mentioned them, and I don't know where they are, or who they are, so I thought it best to say nothing. I suppose I thought that they might have tried to get in touch with me, if only for Emily's sake.'

Ben came to join them, taking a seat beside Sarah on the settee. 'I could see how upset you were just then, when she talked about them, but just because you haven't heard from them, it doesn't necessarily mean that they haven't tried to contact you.'

'Then again, it's possible that something happened to them.' Sarah's mouth wavered. 'Or perhaps there was a family argument. The trouble is, I don't know anything.' She swallowed hard. 'Sometimes I have pictures in my mind, of family life, a big house and a wide driveway, but then it fades and I'm none the wiser. I don't even know if there are one…' Her voice broke. 'Or two sets of grandparents.'

'I can see how that would worry you. It must be so frustrating for you.' Jennifer paused. 'What about Emily's father?' she asked. 'Do you know whether you were married, or perhaps there was a divorce? Does Emily never mention him?'

'I don't…I don't even recall having a child, let alone being married,' Sarah said awkwardly, her voice faltering, 'and Emily has hardly ever talked about her father. It's been difficult to know how to approach the subject with her. She was so shocked by witnessing the attack on me that she clammed up for ages, and we were always afraid of pushing her too far.' She pressed her lips together to stop them from trembling. 'As to whether I was married or divorced, I can't say. When the police found me, they said that there were scratches on my hands. They thought I might have put up a fight against my attacker, and that it was possible I was wearing a ring but that it was stolen.' Her eyes were suddenly blurred by a bright sheen of tears. 'There's no way of knowing.'

Ben put an arm around her, drawing her close to him, as though he would do anything he could to take away her pain. It must have been a purely instinctive action on his part, but it was enough to let her know that he understood what she was going through and that he was concerned enough to want to help her.

'I'm sorry,' he said softly. 'This must be really upsetting for you. It's hard to imagine what it must be like to lose your identity and everything that goes along with it, but you don't have to bear this on your own, you know. We'll do whatever we can to see you through it.'

For a moment or two Sarah gave in to the wonderful feeling of comfort that his nearness evoked. His head rested against hers, and she absorbed the warmth that came from being near him. His arms were strong and capable, and she was sure that he meant what he'd said, and that he would lift any burden from her, given the chance.

Only she couldn't let him do that, could she? He was a neighbour, a new-found friend, a colleague, but he had his own life to lead. No one could bring her family back to her and, when all was said and done, this was her problem.

After a while she began to straighten up. This was something she had to get through on her own. Her life was a mystery, and until the puzzle was solved she had to simply muddle through as best she could.

CHAPTER FIVE

'I MUST be crazy to even think of doing this.' Sarah gazed about her at the rugged landscape, a faint breeze riffling through her hair. In the distance, a river had carved a deep, narrow valley through the grassy plateau, only to disappear underground, following a subterranean course. All around, craggy rocks were exposed, glimpsed through a scattering of woodland. 'I can't begin to know why I let you persuade me to come along with you on this search-and-rescue mission. I don't even like caves.'

'How do you know you don't like them?' Ben looked at her askance. 'You told me you didn't know whether you'd ever been down a cave before.'

'Well, I can't think why anyone would want to let themselves down into the depths of the earth. And I have no idea why Carol was so intent on agreeing with you that this would be a good experience for me. One minute she's telling me that I might not be able to cope on my own with something like moving house, and now she's suggesting that all these new kinds of activities are a wonderful thing.' She glared at him. 'This is all your influence.'

He began to chuckle. 'I seem to have been getting the blame for a lot of what goes on just lately.'

Her glower deepened. 'And are you saying that it isn't your fault?'

'I just happened to mention that trying out lots of new things might be good for you—it might stimulate some part of your memory, and in the end that can only be good, surely?'

Her eyes narrowed, a warning glint sparking to life in them. 'I can't imagine what makes you think that my putting on an oversuit and a helmet and allowing myself to be lowered down into a hole in the rock is going to stimulate any part of my memory, except for the part that tells me this is madness and to get away fast.'

A faint dimple of amusement indented his cheek. 'You forgot to mention the headlamp,' he pointed out.

'Oh, yes, and the fact that it's going to be pitch black down there.' Her face set in an expression of bewildered annoyance. 'What on earth was I thinking?'

'The fact is,' he said in a soothing tone, 'you decided to come along because the paramedics are on hand in this operation and you have your report to write. And you thought that you would be helping someone. If there's one thing I've noticed about you, it's that you're always willing to put yourself out for other people—and the thought of more youngsters being trapped in a cave system was enough to spur you on.'

'Maybe so, but the search-and-rescue team weren't so keen on the idea, were they?'

'They were fine about it once they'd been reassured that I would be responsible for you, and that you were kitted out properly, and knew the basic safety procedures.'

Sarah made a huffing noise, part way between dismissing

the notion that she could ever have been persuaded to be so foolish as to do this and in just a small way allowing that she couldn't in all conscience not do it.

'If I were their parents, I'd want to know that they were only going down there under the supervision of an experienced caver.'

'Maybe so, but you can't govern the actions of young people. The earth is here to be explored, and they have the enthusiasm and the energy to do it.'

'That's why we're here now,' she said bluntly. 'Because they had a great idea, but they appear to have come unstuck.'

'Or stuck, as the case may be.' Ben made a wry smile. 'Some of the tunnels in these caverns can be tight, to say the least, but at any rate one of the boys managed to find his way out and was able to fetch help.'

She threw him another withering glance. 'If we're going to do this, let's get on with it, shall we? Before I change my mind?'

The rescue team began the descent into the cave via a wide fissure in the rock, and Sarah was relieved to find that there were plenty of footholds to help her on the way. Easing herself down into a wide cavern, she finally felt solid rock beneath her feet. From there the team followed a low tunnel where they had to dip their heads to avoid the roof.

The air was dank, and already she could feel the chill of a place that had been hidden from sunlight for aeons. 'How many boys are down here altogether?' she asked.

'There are three of them. According to the lad who made it to the surface, one of them had a fall, and another one was too exhausted to go on. One of the younger boys is lost in a tunnel somewhere.'

Ben shone his torch around, illuminating the rock walls and highlighting the deposits of calcite that glittered like ice all the way along the passage. Further on, there were splashes of colour on the rocks, blue-grey manganese and the orange of iron oxide. 'It's easy to see from all these different fissures how easy it would be to lose your way if you didn't know the caves.'

Sarah nodded. She paused to gaze for a moment at the domed ceiling of the cavern they had entered, and then marvelled at the crystalline splendour of the rock formations. It was like walking into a vast hall, with nooks and crannies all around and barely hidden openings in the limestone that hinted at hidden treasures further on begging to be explored.

'It's a good thing that you seem to know where you're going.' They moved through several of these tunnels for some fifteen minutes, until members of the cave rescue team who were up ahead of them signalled that they had come across the injured teenagers.

Sarah picked her way carefully over loose rubble, wet from a thin stream of water trickling down from somewhere above her head, and entered what turned out to be a huge chamber. At the far end of the cavern she could see a boy sitting on the rock floor, leaning against the magnificent column of a stalagmite, formed over centuries out of mineral deposits from the steady drip of water through the roof of the cavern.

He was clutching his injured foot. Next to him was a younger boy, who appeared to be in a dazed condition. A trickle of blood ran down his temple.

Ben went to the boy with the head injury first of all and set about checking his reflexes. The boy didn't appear to be responding too well to Ben's questions, and Sarah was immediately concerned.

'Is he going to be all right?' she asked in a low voice.

Ben nodded. 'He appears to be suffering from concussion. We'll get him to hospital and keep him under observation. I don't think the fall did any great damage to his head, but we'll send him for an X-ray, to be on the safe side.'

Another member of the rescue team was attending to the second boy. 'I thought I might be able to get myself out of here at a push, if help didn't come,' the youngster said in an anxious tone, 'but I didn't want to leave Matthew and Taylor on their own. Besides, I wasn't sure how much further I would be able to go because of the pain.'

'You did right to stay here, Kieran,' his rescuer told him. 'The ankle is quite swollen, and it's better that you rested it. It's probably just a bad sprain, but we'll know more after the doctor has checked you out at the hospital. In the meantime, we'll wrap a support bandage around the ankle and put it in a splint to protect it from any further damage.'

'Have they found Taylor yet?' Kieran wanted to know. 'He went off to see if he could find a quicker way out of here, but he never came back. We heard him shouting, and we tried to call back, but after a while he went quiet.'

'The men have gone to look for him,' Ben said, glancing around. 'They'll let us know as soon as they find him.'

He went to help his colleague to splint the boy's ankle, while Sarah stayed with the youth who was concussed and feeling sick. She spoke gently to him, wiping his brow with a cool, damp cloth and reassuring him that he was going to be all right and that soon they would have him out of there. A few minutes later two of the rescue team members came back to the cavern.

'We've found the boy wedged in a fissure in the rock up ahead,' he said. 'They're putting a harness around him to make sure that we have him safe, and then we'll have to chisel away some of the rock so that we can ease him out of there. He's lucky that he didn't fall down one of the main shafts.'

'Is he injured in any way?' Ben asked.

'Just some soreness in his leg where it was grazed by the rock, and general exhaustion, but otherwise I think he'll be fine. He's not complaining of problems anywhere else.'

'That's good. Maybe we should start getting Matthew and Kieran out of here. We can send them off to hospital in the first ambulance.'

The other men agreed, and between them they carefully slid the boys onto stretchers and began to retrace their steps to the mouth of the cave system. Kieran was worried about leaving his friend behind, but Sarah said softly, 'He's being well looked after. The men with him know all about taking care of people who are trapped in the caves, and they won't leave him. It might take a while, but they'll bring him out safely.'

When they arrived at the point where they had lowered themselves into the cave system, she stared up at the crooked sides of the pothole. 'How are we going to get them up out of the fissure?' she murmured, glancing at Ben.

'Two of us will have to go up to the surface and drop down the lifting tackle. Then the other two will make sure that the clasps are fitted securely to the stretcher harness and help lift the boys up, one at a time. It could be quite a slow process.'

Sarah frowned. 'Do you always manage to save the people you come to find?' she asked in a low voice.

He nodded. 'We haven't failed yet.' He gave her a quick smile. 'You know, you've done really well today—you seemed to have coped with all the climbing and negotiating the more tricky parts of the tunnels. How do you feel about being down here?'

Her mouth tipped into a crooked grin. 'Do you know, I think I've actually enjoyed it…once I knew that the boys were not seriously hurt. After that I began to relax a bit, and to be honest I think the caves are quite beautiful in an eerie sort of way.'

He laughed. 'That's my girl. I knew that tirade was all steam and hot air when we first set out. I didn't think you would be able to stay mad at me for long.'

By now they were busy organising the stretchers, getting them ready for transfer to the surface. Matthew was the first to be taken up through the narrow passageway, and once he was safely at the surface, Ben came down to retrieve Kieran.

Sarah had stayed behind with the boy. She had already fixed the harness in place on the stretcher, along with a safety rope that she had been instructed to clip to her belt. Ben checked what she had done before pronouncing that everything was in order.

'We'll do this one together,' he said. 'I'll handle this end of the stretcher and you can follow. Just make sure you take your time. You can't come to any harm because we have you fixed to a lead rope on the surface, and I won't be far ahead of you.'

By the time they had finished the manoeuvre, Sarah was on a high of excitement. This was something she had never done before, she was fairly sure of that, but it was one more challenge that she had mastered, and it gave her added confidence to deal with whatever lay ahead.

The ambulance moved off, taking the two boys to hospital, but the rescue team stayed behind to go and lend a hand with freeing the third boy.

It turned out that he was in fairly good shape, though his rescue had taken some two hours.

'Has it put you off caving?' Sarah asked the boy, when they finally had him out in the fresh air once more.

'No way,' he said. 'Only,' he added on a thoughtful note, 'I might think about wearing shinpads next time.'

Sarah laughed. 'Then I guess it's true what they say, that you can't keep a good man down.'

She checked her watch as the ambulance moved away, leaving the rescue team behind. They had been there for the whole of the morning.

'Are you worried about getting back for Emily?' Ben asked.

'A little,' she admitted. 'I know that she'll be all right, because she's been to nursery this morning and Carol was going to pick her up from there for me, but I don't like to leave her for too long. Besides, Carol has taken in another couple of foster-children this last week, and she has her work cut out for her. It sounds as though these new children have had a difficult family life, and it's taking a while for them to settle.'

He nodded. 'We'll be setting off back to the base any minute now, and then I'll take you to pick her up.'

Sarah helped load the rescue tackle into the van, and then took her seat in there beside Ben. One of the team members, Jack, a paramedic in his mid-thirties, turned round to speak to her as the driver started the engine.

'You seemed to have picked things up fairly quickly, considering this was your first time down the caves. It was good to have you along with us, especially when it came to calming the young lads. Do you think you might be coming along with us another time? We could always do with more people to help out.'

'I'll give it some thought,' Sarah said. 'It was certainly a much more stimulating experience than I'd expected.'

Jack grinned. 'You should come along to our charity event at the weekend,' he said. 'We hold it in the community hall every year, and it's a good chance for everyone to get together. If the weather is fine, we have stalls outside in the grounds where people can come and buy stuff. Then, in the evening, there's a dance.'

'That sounds like a major event,' Sarah said.

Jack nodded. 'It is. We usually manage to collect quite a good amount for the rescue team's funds. Do you think you might come and join us?'

Sarah was instantly guarded. 'I'm not sure whether I can make it, but I'll certainly keep it in mind.'

Jack seemed to be reasonably satisfied with that answer, and he turned back to face the front of the vehicle and watch the passing scenery, chatting to the man who was sitting next to him.

Ben wasn't so easy to fob off, and she guessed he had seen through her noncommittal answer right away. 'What do you have on this weekend that's so special?' he said. 'Are you planning on attacking the Aga for the umpteenth time, or have you decided that this is the weekend for you to paint the kitchen now that the damp problem has been sorted out?'

'The cooker is just fine,' she said, going on the defensive, 'but you're right about painting the kitchen. I've already made a start in there. Actually, I thought about putting tiles on the walls. I found some in the shed, still in their boxes, and it looks as if there are enough for me to do the whole area that was affected by the damp. I was going to have a go at scrubbing the old wooden table as well, to see if I could do anything with it, as it's good and solid. Then there's Emily's bedroom to decorate, and that's before I even start on the living room.'

'But the truth is, you could drop all that and go to the charity event instead, couldn't you, if you really wanted to?'

Sarah squirmed in her seat, moving her shoulders in a negligent fashion, hoping that he would drop the subject. 'I really think I need to get the house to rights before I do anything else.'

'Well, here's the thing…how would it be if I were to help you with the decorating and you take a break this weekend to come to the fete and stay on for the dance in the evening?'

Her brows lifted that. 'I really don't think I could let you do that. You work hard enough as it is and the truth is, I don't feel comfortable in crowds. I'd much rather stay away, if it's all the same to you…but thank you anyway for the offer.'

'You've absolutely no idea what you're turning down.' His brows lifted in astonishment at her lack of foresight. 'I'm a dab hand at decorating—I helped my mother do her place up. She didn't want to get people in to do it, and I thought, Well, why not give it a try? As to you not liking crowds, I would be there with you to give you moral support.'

'I don't think so. Thanks, but I'm not ready to start socialising just yet. It's a big enough step for me that I've actually moved into my own place.'

'But it would be good for Emily, wouldn't it?'

She frowned, sensing that he wasn't going to give up easily, and he went on, 'She would love some of the activities that they put on—there are kiddie rides and face painting and all sorts of things that she might want to try.'

She sent him an edgy stare. 'You're certainly persistent, aren't you?'

'If I think something's important enough, yes.'

'It was actually Jack's idea.'

'Ah, but I was planning on asking you about it. Besides, think of the article you could write for the local paper— "Riding out with the Rescue Team—My Ultimate Reward".'

She laughed at that. 'The reward being that I get to attend the dance in the evening?'

He inclined his head a fraction. 'There is that, or the satisfaction of seeing the rescues take place and making sure that the injured are sent to the hospital for treatment.' He thought it through some more. 'You could probably get two articles out of it…one, an account of the rescue team's mission to bring out the injured boys, and, two, a piece on the fete and how they need extra funds.'

She fixed him with her blue gaze. 'You make a habit of this, don't you?'

'A habit of what? I'm not sure that I'm following you.'

'Of trying to get me to do things that I don't want to do. You seem to have it down to a fine art.' She made a face. 'I say, "No, thanks," so you say, "Ah, but what if?" and whatever I say from then on, you come up with a way of countering all my objections.'

He nodded. 'That sounds like a fairly reasonable explanation to me.' He studied her. 'So you may as well give in right away and save yourself the bother of arguing. I'll come and pick you up at lunchtime on Saturday, shall I?'

She started to smile. 'I'll think about it.'

A few minutes later they were dropped off at the rescue team's base, and from there Ben drove her to pick up Emily.

'How has she been?' Sarah asked. 'Did nursery go all right?'

'She had a great time as usual,' Carol said. 'I took my two latest foster-children along with me when I went to pick her up, but I'm not altogether sure that that was a good idea. Perhaps I ought to have left them with Tom.'

'Why is that?' Sarah frowned. Carol was looking a little strained, and that wasn't like her at all. 'Have you had some trouble?'

'No, it was nothing like that. It's just that my two little people have had a few problems settling in, and they've been a bit fractious. Emily's so sweet-natured I think she found it all a bit confusing, to be honest.'

Ben was listening with interest. 'Are they likely to be with you for long?'

Carol frowned. 'I'm not sure. The mother is ill in hospital, and the father isn't really able to cope on his own. I think he and his wife were having a few problems, and now he's struggling to come to terms with her being sick.'

'It sounds as though you're having to pick up the pieces,' Ben murmured.

Carol nodded.

'Is there anything that I can do to help?' Sarah asked. 'I could have them over to play with Emily for a while, if you like?'

'Perhaps in a week or so, when they've settled down a bit,' Carol murmured. 'That would be good. Thanks.'

Emily appeared to have put her confusion behind her as she ran out to Ben's car. 'I painted a picture today,' she said. 'I done it with my hands…look.'

Sarah and Ben both looked at the palms she held out to them. There were purple smudges mixed with a tinge of green that had obviously withstood the attempt of the teacher to wash it away.

'Well, that must have been some picture,' Ben said in an appreciative tone.

'Green and purple—I can't wait to see it when it's dried out and they let you bring it home,' Sarah murmured. 'It will go so well with the colours in the kitchen.'

Emily sent them a contented smile.

Over the next couple of days, Sarah concentrated on her work for the newspaper and on writing up the first part of her report for the ambulance service. In the evenings, when Emily was tucked up in bed, she made a start on scrubbing the wooden table in the kitchen, trying to restore it to its former glory.

Ben must have decided to come and lend a hand despite her protests, because he arrived one evening armed with tile cement and tile cutters, looking as though he was ready for action.

'I'll make a start in the kitchen, shall I?' he asked. 'The wall seems to have dried out well enough, and from what you showed me the other day, you have enough tiles to finish the job.'

'I didn't take you seriously when you said that you would help with the decorating,' Sarah said. 'I'm sure you have far better things to do with your time.'

'I can't think of any at the moment,' he said. He looked at the table that she had been working on. 'That's looking really good, isn't it? Are you thinking of finishing it off with a coat of wax? I think varnish would spoil it, don't you?'

'I'm not sure. I only seem to be able to think one step at a time at the moment.'

'That's fine.' He glanced meaningfully at the kettle. 'A cup of tea would go down really well.'

She made the tea, and after that they worked together in harmony for a couple of hours or so. Sarah had another go at bringing the wooden table to its once pristine condition and then did a final buffing up of the Aga, before cleaning up and going to check on Emily.

When she came downstairs a few minutes later, the wall that had been such a sore point was beautifully finished with tiles, lending a whole new aspect to her vision of a farmhouse kitchen. Ben was washing his hands at the kitchen sink.

'It looks lovely,' she said, her mouth dropping open a fraction in wonder. She stared at his handiwork in awe. 'You've made a wonderful job of it.'

'I'm glad that you think so,' he murmured, coming to stand beside her. He slid an arm around her waist. 'At this rate, we should soon have the cottage looking like a proper home.'

She sent him a quizzical look. 'You weren't thinking of doing any more work on it, were you?'

'I did say that I would decorate Emily's room for you, didn't I?' He smiled down at her. 'That's something to be left for the daytime, though, and it will have to wait until I get a day off from work.'

'You've done so much for me already. Just getting the landlord to agree to fix the damp was enough.' She was discovering that she liked having his arm around her. It made her feel warm and safe, as though, while she was in his arms, nothing bad could happen to her. For the first time in months she felt as though life was something to be treasured because there were people around her who made a difference to the way she looked at things. Above all, Ben made her feel glad that she was a woman, and stirred up emotions within her that she scarcely recognised. It was as though her whole body glowed from within.

She looked at him. 'Thank you for helping me this way.'

'It was my pleasure,' he murmured. His glance meshed with hers, then drifted down to take in the full, soft curve of her lips. Slowly he bent his head towards her and what happened next was as inevitable as birdsong filling the air on a new day.

His mouth brushed hers, lightly testing its sweetly yielding softness, and then that gentle exploration deepened into a kiss that turned her blood to pure flame. A thrill of sensation swept through her like wildfire, filling her whole body with elation, and when his palm flattened on her spine and urged her closer to him, she went willingly.

She loved the way the softness of her curves melded with the taut strength of his body, and she craved the touch of his hands as he slid them over the fullness of her hips.

'I can't imagine why I haven't done this before,' he said, his voice thick. 'It feels so good, holding you this way.'

She moved against him, a breathy sigh breaking in her throat as she savoured the heady swirl of delight that came from being in his embrace. It was as though she had hungered for him, as though this enveloping warmth, this feeling that she had finally come home was what she had been waiting for all these long, difficult months since her life had been jump-started back at the hospital.

His hands moved over her, tracing the gentle curve of her back, shifting to draw her up against the strong muscles of his thighs. His cheek grazed hers, and his lips trailed over the smooth line of her temple.

'You make me feel dizzy with excitement,' she whispered, 'as though the whole world is spinning round.'

He looked down at her. 'Are you all right?' A thread of concern ran through his words.

'I'm fine,' she murmured. 'Why shouldn't I be? I feel as though I've drunk too much wine.' She looked up at him and gave a husky laugh. 'I don't remember ever doing that. Do you think I'm having a flashback?'

He gently eased her from him and steadied her with his hands on her shoulders. 'I think you might have been overdoing things. Perhaps I've pushed you too far lately. I should remember that you've been ill.'

'That was a long time ago.' She pulled in a deep breath, the euphoria of the last few moments slowly beginning to fade, only to be replaced by a muzzy sensation that swirled through her head. For a few brief moments she had forgotten all about the fact that she had been in hospital, that she had lived an entirely different existence from the one she was living now.

What was she thinking of, kissing Ben? How could she be sure that there wasn't someone waiting for her somewhere, someone who cared about her and needed her to be by his side?

Ben looked into her eyes, and perhaps he was coming to that very same realisation because he became still all at once, and his gaze was troubled.

'Sarah, I should have—'

'No, it's all right.' She stopped him before he could say anything more. She didn't want to talk about that other life right now, or even to acknowledge aloud that it existed. Instead, she said quietly, 'There can't be anything wrong with me if I've been able to make a start on renovating this place, can there?'

'That's true.' He must have known that she was trying to backtrack from that tender, wonderful kiss. He made no attempt to bring her back into his arms, and he seemed ready enough to accept her change of conversation.

His expression was serious. 'You're doing well, but I'll do the bulk of the work from now on, and if there are things I can't find time for, I'll bring someone in to do it.'

She shook her head. 'No, I can't let you do that. This is something I need to do for myself, and I have to take my time with it. I can't afford to get it done all at once.'

'You don't need to worry about that.'

She frowned. 'Why not?' It was as though those moments of closeness had never been, and she felt out of place, out of synch with everything that was going on.

'Because I've signed the contract to buy this place, so it means that I'm your new landlord. It's my job to see that it's fit to be lived in, and I take that responsibility seriously.'

She made a soft sound of disbelief in the back of her throat. It was as though he had winded her with his statement. He was the new landlord?

'Does that mean that you get to say what changes will be made? Will I have no say in how I want things to be done?'

'Of course you'll have a say. Everything's as it was before, except that I'll be the one overseeing the work.'

She reached for a chair and sat down, all the stuffing knocked out of her. So he hadn't come here this evening simply to be with her and help her with the renovations? He had come to do the work because he felt obliged to carry out his duties as a landlord, and the fact that he had kissed her didn't signify anything. It meant only that he had been carried away by the sheer exhilaration of a job well done, and she had happened to be on hand to share in that.

Disillusionment swept over her. 'I had no idea,' she said, bracing herself to deal with this new shock. She felt foolish. Above all, she didn't want him to know that she had been in any way affected by that sudden rush of passion. It was over and done with, and it had to stand as a warning to her not to give way to her emotions in the future.

It was one of the things they had warned her about after the head injury. 'You might suffer from mood swings and un-expected bouts of weepiness or emotional instability,' the doctor had said.

That was definitely one warning she would take to heart from this point on. Her judgement was obviously flawed, and she had to learn to keep her instincts in check.

'Things will go on as they did before,' Ben was saying. 'Choose the wallpaper you want for the living room and bedroom and I'll see to it that the job's done for you.'

'Thanks,' she said. 'I'll bear it in mind.'

He looked at her oddly, and perhaps it was the clipped tone she had used that made him pause for thought. He didn't comment, though, except to say, 'You're tired, aren't you? It must have been a long day for you, with one thing and another. I'll leave you to get yourself to bed.' He hesitated, and then added with a wry tilt to his mouth, 'Unless you need a hand to do that?'

She stood up, throwing him an inhibiting stare. 'I expect I'll see you in the morning,' she said, going over to the kitchen door and opening it. 'Goodnight, Ben.'

''Night, Sarah.'

CHAPTER SIX

'ARE you ready to go?' There was a tinge of doubt in Ben's tone as his glance flickered over Sarah from head to toe.

Bleary eyed, she gazed at him over the rim of her coffee-cup. Why was he looking at her like that? Did he think she looked a mess? She was wearing khaki-coloured cargo trousers, her favourites because they had a multitude of pockets that she found useful when she was out and about, and a cotton T-shirt that was comfortable and fitted really well.

'I think so.' She frowned. 'You're early this morning, aren't you?' She looked down at her watch, but the attempt to focus was too much for her and she gave up on the attempt. 'I've only just come back from dropping Emily off at nursery.'

'No. I'm bang on time.' He frowned. 'Perhaps you're not firing on all cylinders today?'

A line indented her brow as she mulled that over. He probably had a point there. She felt decidedly under par, whereas he was his usual energetic, lively self, ready to deal with whatever the day threw at him. He even looked good. Even in her befuddled state, she was able to take in the fact that he was a sight for sore eyes. That dark hair, and those sculpted, angular features were enough to make any woman go weak at the knees.

She tried to shake off the hazy yearnings and the aching despair of unfulfilled need that suddenly welled up inside her. Whatever it was that she wanted, she knew better than to look in his direction. He was off limits and, no matter what she felt for him, she had to remember that she might be spoken for.

'I'll be all right just as soon as I've finished my coffee. Do you want to sit down for a minute?' She waved a hand towards a chair by the kitchen table.

'No, thanks. We have a callout—someone who has fallen from a roof he was working on, and his workmate is suffering from shock and bruising because he was on a ladder beneath him and was knocked to the ground. The ambulance is already on its way.'

'Oh… I see…' She put down her coffee-cup. 'In that case…' She searched around for her bag, and gazed blankly at the empty space where it should have been.

'Is this what you're looking for?' Ben asked, lifting her bag from the Welsh dresser and handing it to her.

'Um…yes. Thanks.' She made a brief check inside the bag to make sure that she had her notebook and a pen. 'OK, I'm ready.'

She went out with him to the rapid-response car, and once they were settled inside, Ben started off in the direction of the callout. He wound down the windows, letting a blast of fresh air fill the vehicle, and she guessed that he was doing what he could to ensure that she was fully awake.

'So what happened?' he asked. 'Did you have a late night?'

'It wasn't so much late as disturbed,' she told him. 'Emily has been having bad dreams recently, and last night was particularly bad. I had to go in and reassure her on several occasions. It won't matter for her, because she can have a nap at nursery if she wants, but I'm having trouble keeping my eyes open this morning.'

'So that's why you needed the coffee.' He gave a faint smile. 'Perhaps the fresh air will perk you up a bit.'

'Let's hope so.' She gazed out of the window, not really taking in the undulating landscape but trying to focus her mind on what lay ahead.

'What's causing Emily to have these bad dreams? Do you know?'

'I'm not altogether sure.' Sarah frowned, trying to piece together what had been going on. 'I think it's something to do with the children that Carol is fostering. I suppose it could be that she's feeling a little jealous of the attention they're getting. I can't quite work it out, and she isn't very clear as to what she's dreaming about. When I go to her when she wakes up in the night, she's very confused. She sometimes shouts things out, but none of it makes any sense.'

'Do you think it could be that she's remembering the day that you were attacked? It must have been very frightening for her to see her mother in such a helpless situation.'

Sarah's mouth flattened. 'I don't know. Apparently she said very little about it when it first happened. Then, when I came out of hospital, we encouraged her to tell us what she was thinking, to no avail, but she seemed to be doing better, and we thought that she had brushed it off, in the way that children do forget these things.'

'Hmm. I suppose moving house might have been enough to stir things up again.'

Sarah nodded, sending him a bleak look. 'I feel guilty

about that, but it was something I felt I had to do, and sooner or later we would have had to leave Carol's house anyway. We couldn't be a burden on them for much longer. But initially it seemed that Emily took the move in her stride.'

He shot her a quick glance. 'You shouldn't blame yourself. Children are very resilient, and I dare say she'll come through this well enough.'

By the time they arrived at their destination, Sarah was feeling much more like her normal self. The paramedics were already attending to the man who had fallen from the roof, although he was still lying on the ground, while his colleague was sitting on the steps at the back of the ambulance. Sarah guessed that he was being treated for shock.

Already, a small crowd of onlookers had gathered across the road. It looked to Sarah as though they were mostly people who had come out of the shop opposite to see what was going on, and some had come out of their houses, probably to see if there was anything they could do to help.

She turned her attention back to the injured men. 'He's not able to move his arm because of extreme pain,' the paramedic was saying to Ben. 'Otherwise he has swelling around his shoulder and skin abrasions. He's fully conscious.'

Ben knelt down to examine the patient. 'Do you have pain anywhere else, John?' he asked. 'Try to keep your head and spine as still as possible, until we can get you on to the stretcher.'

'It's hard to say,' John mumbled. 'The shoulder's the worst. That took the brunt of the fall.'

'Yes, I think you've probably broken your shoulder blade—I'll immobilise it by putting a sling in place, and I'll give you something for the pain.' Before he did that, though,

Ben assessed the man's response to stimulation by pressing on various parts of his legs.

Then he spoke to the paramedic, and they had a brief conversation about how they were going to move the patient. 'We'll need everyone to work together to lift him as carefully as possible.'

Turning back to the man, he said, 'I'm going to put a collar round your neck to make sure that we keep everything perfectly still, and after that we're going to put you onto a spinal board, just to make sure that you don't suffer any more damage. You'll be checked over more thoroughly for other injuries at the hospital.'

Sarah helped to lift the man onto the spinal board, and then stood back as Ben and the paramedics prepared to strap him in place.

A few minutes later he was safely in the ambulance, and the vehicle moved away, taking him to the hospital. Sarah watched until it was out of sight, and wondered how he would fare.

Several more calls followed during the course of the morning, and she busied herself noting down all the aspects of care that would go into her report.

'Are you managing to get all the information you need?' Ben asked. 'I know it can be difficult when you're not familiar with the equipment and you may not be sure how it's used.'

'I haven't had any trouble so far,' Sarah told him. 'The paramedics have helped me out with one or two things that I wasn't sure of, but for the most part I seem to be managing.' She moved her shoulders, easing a knot of tension that had formed there.

Ben observed the action. 'I think it's time we stopped for

lunch,' he murmured. 'We could buy something from the local bakery, if you like?'

'That sounds like a good idea.' She glanced around. 'Aren't we fairly close to where your mother lives? You could perhaps go and look in on her if you wanted, and then come back to pick me up later.'

'Or you could come with me.' He raised a questioning brow. 'I'm sure she would like to see you again.'

'OK, if you think she won't mind.'

They bought crispy bread rolls with cheese and salad fillings, along with iced buns and chocolate eclairs for dessert, and Sarah felt her mouth already watering with anticipation.

'I didn't realise that I was so hungry,' she murmured.

'You're lucky that you can eat chocolate eclairs and buns without having to worry about putting on weight,' Ben commented, his glance skimming over her slight figure.

Sarah fidgeted under that assessing gaze. 'That's not exactly true,' she said. 'My appetite appears to have improved lately, and I've actually put on a few pounds.'

His grey eyes took on a smoky glimmer. 'It suits you. You look lovely, very appealing, with curves in all the right places.'

Sarah felt her face run with heat, but he just laughed softly and held open the door of the car so that she could slide in.

When they arrived at his mother's house just a short time later, it was clear that Jennifer was more than happy to see them.

'I was wondering how you were getting on with your new job,' she told Sarah, as she showed them into the kitchen. 'Ben told me that you had been out with the cave rescue team. That must have been quite an experience for you.' She busied herself filling the kettle with water and setting out plates on the dining table.

'It was, but, then, I seem to have been doing all sorts of things that I've never done before. Just being on call with the paramedics takes me out and about all over the place, sometimes further afield than you might imagine, especially if we're transporting a patient between hospitals.'

'I expect it does.' Jennifer studied Sarah for a moment. 'Has it stirred any memories for you? Have there been any places that you recognised?'

Sarah nodded cautiously. 'I wasn't sure, but there was a stretch of land that looked vaguely familiar. There was a farmhouse, set in a deep valley, with a few isolated cottages here and there. It was just a fleeting thing, though, and I couldn't have said that I specifically remember it as something from my past. As far as I know, I was expecting to travel further north before I was attacked. I suppose it could have been that I visited the area as a child.'

Ben sent her a quick glance. 'This whole region is a magnet for tourists, and if you lived further away it's possible that you came here once in a while. I'm sure it will come to you, given time. Sometimes these things are more likely to happen when you're feeling relaxed, and you haven't had a chance to simply sit back and absorb things, have you?' He waved her to a chair, and began to set the food out on plates.

'I bought cheese and salad rolls for you,' he told his mother, 'and there are iced buns and chocolate eclairs for afterwards. I know how much you like them.'

Jennifer gave a pleased smile. 'I do. It was so thoughtful of you to do that.' She stopped to pull in a breath or two, and then sat down, needing to rest for a moment.

Ben finished making a pot of tea and then came to join them at the table. 'I've been trying to persuade Sarah that she should come along to the rescue team's fundraising dance tomorrow. I think it would do her some good. Like I said, she needs to relax a bit.'

Jennifer paused in the act of biting into her cheese roll. 'You will go to it, won't you?' she said looking at Sarah. 'I know that people have a lot of fun there.'

'I am not sure about that,' Sarah murmured. 'I'll take Emily along to the fete, but the evening's a bit more tricky. There's always a problem of finding a babysitter.' It was an excuse, but it was also true.

'I could do it for you,' Jennifer said. 'I would love to take care of Emily for you.'

Sarah opened her mouth to say something, but Ben interrupted before she could answer. 'I don't think that would be wise,' he said. 'You may be feeling better in yourself, but you're still not as strong as you were, and two-year-olds can be challenging at the best of times. Even Sarah gets exhausted looking after her.'

'I think you're worrying too much,' Jennifer told him, but Ben was adamant.

'Anyway,' he said, 'I'm sure Emily's foster-mother would be only too happy to have Emily for a few hours. She said as much to me when I spoke to her about it the other day.'

Sarah's eyes widened. 'You spoke to her about it? When was this?'

'A few days ago, when the subject of the dance first came up. I think you were talking to Emily and the new foster-children, at the time. Carol thought going to the dance would do you a world of good.'

Sarah's expression fluctuated between exasperation and amusement.

'It's very thoughtful of you and Carol to consider my well-being that way,' she said in a mock annoyed tone, 'but you have to remember that I was in hospital because I had an injury to my brain… I didn't have my brain removed while I was there, and I am capable of making decisions for myself, you know.'

Jennifer began to laugh. 'She has a point there, Ben.'

He acknowledged that with a faint tilt to his mouth. 'I appreciate that,' he said, looking at Sarah, 'but you haven't taken any time for yourself, and I think you should.'

Sarah sent him a stare. At least his mother understood how she felt.

Some time later, Jennifer saw them out of the front door as they readied themselves to return to work. She came outside with them to the front of the house, stopping to say a few words to her neighbour, who was busy deadheading flowers in her garden.

Ben introduced Sarah to the neighbour and pointed out her small child, Ryan, a boy of about three, who was kneeling down and running a toy car along the path.

'Jane's been keeping an eye on my mother while she's been ill. She's been a terrific help to us, and she's managed to take a lot of the worry from me.'

'I can imagine.'

The neighbour chatted to Ben and his mother for a short time, and Sarah contented herself with listening and glancing over to the little boy from time to time. He stood up and disappeared round a corner of the house, but after a while he reappeared, surreptitiously holding something in one hand, while trailing the car along the top of an ornamental birdbath with the other.

As she watched, he tripped over the raised edging of the path and fell to the ground. Sarah was ready to go over to him to make sure that he was all right, but after a moment he stood up and stayed very still. His back was to her, and it occurred to Sarah that there was something strange about the way he was simply standing there, but it might have been that he was taking time to plan what he was going to do next.

His mother was still talking to Ben and Jennifer, and Sarah guessed that she had not seen him fall. Perhaps she ought to mention it to her in case he had grazed his knee?

Then, all at once, as she watched, the child's legs seemed to buckle under him and he collapsed to the ground. Sarah gave a small cry of dismay and ran towards him, kneeling down and turning him over. He was limp in her arms, and there was a bluish tinge to his mouth. His eyes appeared to be rolling back in his head.

Sarah wasn't sure what to do. Was he having a fit? Then, as she looked him over, she saw that he had the remains of a biscuit clutched in his hand. Swiftly, she opened his mouth and looked to see if there was anything in there. At the back of his throat she saw a small portion of biscuit that had remained whole, and without giving it any more thought she started to tug on it with her fingers. It came free, but he still remained limp in her arms, and in desperation she turned him over and thumped his back.

By now Ben had come to kneel beside her, and she was aware of the boy's mother looking on in agonised dismay. She was half expecting Ben to take over from her, but he didn't, and she wondered if he thought that she knew what she was doing. The truth was, she didn't. She had acted without thinking at all.

After what seemed like an endless minute, Ryan spluttered, and what was left of the biscuit dropped out of his mouth onto the grass. Sarah breathed a sigh of relief. Bringing him back into a half-sitting position, she examined him to make sure he was breathing.

The little boy opened his eyes and lay there for a moment, looking up at her.

Then he frowned, and in a grumpy voice he muttered, 'Where's my biscuit?' and all the while he was staring at her as though she had been responsible for stealing it from him.

Sarah didn't know whether to laugh or cry. 'You had me so worried just then, young man,' she said.

'Oh, thank heaven,' his mother said. She reached for him and Sarah relinquished the child into his mother's arms. Jane was hugging him at the same time as scolding him for sneaking into the house to find the biscuits. 'Ryan, don't you ever do that to me again,' she told him.

She looked up at Sarah. 'I don't know how to thank you,' she said. 'You saved his life.'

'I'm just glad that he's all right,' Sarah murmured. After a while, she turned to Ben and Jennifer. 'Did I hear the bleeper a moment ago?'

Ben nodded. 'We have another callout.' He smiled. 'At the time I thought what you were doing was too important to drag you away.'

She returned the smile. 'It looks as though he's going to be all right, doesn't it?'

'It does, thanks to you.' He slid an arm around her and gave her a gentle squeeze. 'You did exactly the right thing.'

Sarah basked in the warmth of his touch for a second or two, but then he released her and the feeling of being safe and cherished dissolved as rapidly as it had formed.

'What a blessing that you were both here,' Jennifer said. She laid a hand lightly on Sarah's arm. 'Don't leave it too long before you visit me again. And let me know how you get on at the dance.' There was a twinkle in her eye as she said it, and Sarah smiled wryly. What chance did she have of ever being independent when everyone she knew was gathering forces against her?

The next day, as it turned out, was a huge success. Emily loved every minute of it, clapping her hands together in delight at the antics of the puppets in the marionette show and waving happily as she steered her racing car on the fairground roundabout.

Ben stayed with them throughout the whole of the afternoon, guiding them through the maze of activities and keeping Emily amused while Sarah explored the delights of the craft stall and the flower tent.

'There are so many people here,' Sarah said, looking around her in amazement as they sat at a table in the refreshments area. 'This whole thing must have taken such a lot of organisation. Did you have a hand in it?'

'I arranged for some of the stallholders to come and sell their goods,' he said, 'and I contacted the people who are providing the refreshments. We're lucky that the weather's holding out, given that it has been raining off and on just lately. It would have been a shame to have to take everything indoors.'

'Yes, it would.' She took a sip of her ice-cold drink. 'This is delicious.'

'It's good to see you looking as though you're enjoying yourself,' Ben said. He watched her for a long moment. 'You have a beautiful smile, and we don't see nearly enough of it. Today has been different, though, and I'm glad of that. It's the first time I've seen you free from worry and able to sit back and unwind.'

'I'm glad that I let you talk me into coming.' She watched as Emily played on the grass beside her with one of the toys that she had bought for her from the toy stall. 'Emily's had a wonderful time, and I was especially happy to see that Carol and Tom were able to come along with their two new charges.'

He nodded. 'I saw Carol being tugged over to the karate display an hour or so ago. Young James was determined that they should watch the performance.'

Sarah's expression softened. 'I think she's really taken to those two but, even so, she's hoping that the parents will sort themselves out once the mother has been released from hospital, and that the children will be able to go back to them before too long.'

Ben nodded. 'It can't be an easy job, fostering children.'

They finished their drinks and wandered about the meadow for another half an hour or so, looking at the stalls they had missed earlier. All too soon, though, the afternoon came to an end.

'What did you like best of all?' Sarah asked Emily as they walked towards the car park.

'I liked Ben giving me a ride on his shoulders,' Emily said. She looked up at Ben and held out her arms, ready to be picked up. ' 'Nother one.'

Ben grinned down at her and obliged with good humour. 'You like being as tall as a giant, don't you?'

'Yes,' Emily said gleefully.

They met up with Carol and Tom in the field that served as a car park. 'Emily can come back home with us,' Carol said. 'She likes playing with James and Katie, and they love having her around. I wish I could keep her with us overnight, but I don't have the room now that I have these two little ones.' She looked fondly at the boy and girl who were around four and five years old, and who were busy just then, playing chase with Emily.

'I'll settle her down on the couch in the dining-room when she gets sleepy, and you can fetch her when you come home from the dance,' Carol added. 'It shouldn't disrupt her too much if I dress her ready for bed before she goes to sleep. I have a spare set of pyjamas for her at home. You can just wrap her up in a blanket and take her out to the car. I doubt she'll wake up after all the activity she's had today.'

Sarah didn't have the heart to disagree. It appeared that Carol was looking forward to having Emily stay with her, and any objections she might have had about going to the dance were rapidly being knocked for six. Besides, now that she was in such a carefree mood, the thought of an evening out was becoming more appealing by the minute.

She kissed Emily and waved at her as Carol and Tom set off for home. Then Ben drove her back to the cottage, dropping her off there with a promise that he would be back to pick her up in time to take her to the hall where the dance was being held.

As soon as he had gone, she began to have a change of heart. Why was she doing this? Had she ever been to a dance before?

And what was she going to wear? Her wardrobe was sparse, with just a few choice items that she thought might cover every occasion. Evening-wear hadn't really come into her line of thought when she was shopping.

In the end she picked out a pretty top that was made of a filmy, floaty material, printed in soft pastels, and that swirled as she moved about. Teamed with a plain skirt, she thought it would do reasonably well.

She soaked for a while in a bath full of scented bubbles, hoping that it would soothe her and help her to prepare for the evening, and she washed her hair, although on reflection that seemed to have been a mistake.

Her already unruly curls became even more wild and un-manageable, and by the time she was dressed and ready to apply the finishing touches to her make-up, her nerves were beginning to get the better of her.

The doorbell rang, and she abandoned her attempt to tame her shoulder-length hair and went to answer it.

'Uh…' Ben didn't move a muscle. He stood on the doorstep looking as though he was stunned, and she stared at him in an abstracted fashion for a moment or two.

'What's wrong?' She quickly checked her top to see that everything was in place. 'Am I wearing the wrong thing?' Then she lifted a hand to her hair. 'Or is it my hair? I can't get it to do what I want it to do.'

He still wasn't speaking, but was just standing there, letting his gaze wander over her, and so she said in a husky voice, 'We can forget the whole idea, if you like. There's no reason why you shouldn't go on your own.'

'I wouldn't dream of it,' he said, finding his voice at last. 'You *will* go to the ball, Cinders. You look fantastic, like some beautiful angel that has just floated down to earth in answer to all my prayers.'

She pressed a hand to her throat. 'I don't believe you for a minute, but thanks all the same. I'm a bundle of nerves, and I don't know why.'

He came into the house and laid his hands on her bare arms, sending a tingle of sensation running through her. 'You should believe me,' he said. 'You always look good, but right now you are exquisite. As for the nerves, it's probably because tonight is one more experience that you've forgotten you ever had. I'll be with you all evening, and it will be just fine, you'll see. We'll raid the buffet and drink the wine—well, you will, but I have to stay sober because I'm driving—and we'll dance the night away.'

It turned out exactly as he said it would. The hall had been cleared for dancing, with a dais at one end for the group that was playing the music and buffet tables arranged all along one side. At the far end of the room, tables and chairs had been set out where people could sit and eat.

The music was lively, inviting people to get up and dance, and that's what they did. In between dances, Ben introduced her to his friends from the hospital and to people from the cave rescue team that she had not met before, and it wasn't as difficult as she had half feared. She liked his friends, and it was good talking to them.

'Come dance with me,' he said, late in the evening, taking her by the hand and leading her out once more onto the polished floor. The tempo of the music changed, and he drew her into his arms so that they swayed together with the beat, their feet moving to the rhythm, and Sarah forgot all about anything else. All that mattered was that she was in his arms, feeling the warmth of his body close to hers.

Under the muted lights it seemed as though they were in

another world, and when Ben lowered his head and let his lips trail across her cheek, it seemed as though it was right, as though this was how it should be.

Perhaps the wine she had drunk had gone to her head because it felt as though the two of them were enclosed in an invisible force field where nothing could get through to them.

Ben's hand lightly stroked the curve of her hip. Her whole body burned in response, and she wanted nothing more than to move closer to him, if that were possible.

'This feels so good,' he said, his lips gently nuzzling her throat. 'I love holding you this way.' He smiled. 'You move with the music as though it's part of you.'

'I've always liked this song,' she murmured. 'It's lilting and dreamy and it makes me feel as though I'm walking on air.' Sharing it with Ben was what made it special, though. She couldn't recall ever dancing this way with anyone else.

But she must have done at one time, surely? She must have shared her life with someone who had been special to her, because she had Emily to show for it. What had become of that man?

The music came to an end, and she stood for a moment, trying to work out what it was that would resolve her problems. She felt Ben's glance drift over her, but if he sensed her sudden withdrawal, he chose not to mention it.

The evening drew to a close, and gradually the crowd dispersed. Ben took her to Carol's house so that she could collect Emily, and when they finally arrived back at the cottage, he carried the sleeping child up to her room and laid her down on her bed.

Ben stepped back so that Sarah could draw the covers

over her daughter and lightly kiss her cheek. 'Sleep well, sunbeam.' She stroked Emily's soft, honey curls and then she quietly left the room.

They went downstairs, and Sarah made coffee, sitting down with Ben in the kitchen that was still warm from the heat of the Aga. 'I put it on just to heat the place up,' she said. 'I like sitting in the kitchen, now that it's been spruced up.'

He nodded. 'It's like being in a farmhouse, with all the golden-coloured wood and the bright colours of crockery placed here and there, on the dresser and on shelves. You even have the smell of freshly baked bread in here.'

She gave him a smile. 'That's because I made some this morning. I thought I would put the Aga to the test, and it worked perfectly. You should try some.' She stood up, fetched the loaf from the bread bin and cut a slice for him to sample, spreading it with creamy butter.

He studied her for a moment as she pushed the plate towards him, as though he was about to say something, but thought better of it. 'Thanks.' Tasting the bread, he nodded appreciatively. 'It's good, very good. You must have learned to cook at your mother's knee.'

The image of a woman flashed across Sarah's mind, a woman with tawny hair and blue eyes the colour of the sky on a spring day. Sarah stood by the table, rooted to the spot. She could see her in a kitchen, taking cakes from the oven. 'No, they're too hot for you to eat now,' the woman had said with a smile. 'Wait a little, until they've cooled down.'

'Are you all right?' Ben wiped his hands on a sheet of kitchen towel and came to stand beside her. 'Have you re-membered something?'

'I think so.' Shocked by the strength of the image, she

made to put a hand on the table to steady herself, but Ben reached for her, holding her close.

'Tell me,' he said.

'It was my mother.' Sarah's voice wavered. 'I saw her clearly, as though she was standing here.'

'That's good. It's wonderful that it happened,' Ben said, his hands clasped around her arms as though he feared she might fall. 'It may not seem like it now, because it was so sudden and you're confused, but it means that those memories are still there, albeit that they're hidden away somewhere.'

She felt her legs giving way beneath her, and he eased her down into a chair.

'Something happened at the dance, too, didn't it?' he asked. 'You were having a good time, and then all at once you became very quiet and it seemed as though you had something on your mind.'

'Yes.' She frowned. 'I was happy, and everything was so much better than I had expected, and I don't know what it was that cut across my thoughts, but suddenly I had an odd sensation sweep through me. I felt sure that there must have been someone else in my life…someone who played a big part…' She broke off, not knowing how to go on.

His eyes darkened. 'Like a husband, you mean?'

She nodded. Perhaps the notion of a husband would have comforted her at one time, in that wasteland where she had been before she had met Ben and come to feel close to him. Now, though, the very idea held her heart in an iron vice and she didn't know what she was supposed to do or think.

He hunkered down beside her, looking at her directly, holding her gaze. 'It could be that there never was a husband. Women do sometimes have children without being married after all, and you're not wearing a ring. Whatever the police say about the fact that you might have been wearing one is all supposition.'

Her eyes were troubled. 'But Emily must have a father somewhere.'

'Then why wasn't he with you when you started on your journey with her?'

'I don't know.' Her hands clenched into fists of frustration. 'There's so much that I don't know.'

Just then a faint cry came from upstairs. It was a sob, and then a wail, and Sarah felt her heart turn over.

'Emily's still having bad dreams,' she said. 'I must go to her.'

Ben stood up and moved to one side so that she could go to her child. She hurried up the stairs and pushed open the door to Emily's room. The little girl was sitting up in bed, her face streaked with tears, and when she saw Sarah she held out her arms to her.

'Daddy gone away,' she cried. 'Daddy gone.'

Sarah put her arms around her and hugged her tight, rocking to and fro and gently soothing her as best she could. 'I'm here,' she said. 'Tell me all about it.'

Emily rubbed her eyes with her knuckles. 'Mummy... Mummy poorly.'

Sarah felt her throat constrict. Had Ben been right when he'd suggested that seeing her mother being attacked had lain dormant in Emily's mind? How could she help a two-year-old to say what was troubling her? She was working in a fog, unless Emily was to say more, to add something that would give her a clue as to what their lives had been before the attack.

But after that Emily was quiet. She didn't say anything, but hiccuped softly, tiny little sobbing sounds in the back of her throat that gradually dwindled away as Sarah held her. After a while her tiny body relaxed, and Sarah realised that she must have fallen asleep.

She glanced round and saw that Ben was standing in the doorway, silently watching her. 'Is she asleep?' he mouthed, and Sarah nodded.

Carefully, so as not to disturb her, she laid Emily down and settled the covers around her once more.

Ben walked with her down the stairs. 'At least now you know what it is that's bothering her,' he said on a flat note.

Sarah nodded. 'But I don't have the first idea how to put it right.'

He put his arms around her and laid a light kiss on her forehead, and for a moment they stayed like that, entwined, drawing succour from each other. They both knew that it was a comfort kiss, a way of saying that he was there to lend his support, because how could it be anything more than that?

CHAPTER SEVEN

'Can we go park today, Mummy? I want to go on the swings.' Emily spooned cereal into her mouth, and then waved the spoon about to emphasise how much she wanted to go out. 'I really, really want to go park.'

'And I would like to take you,' Sarah said, 'but it's starting to rain.'

Emily pressed her lips together in an expression that meant trouble was brewing. ''Tisn't.' She looked at Sarah as though daring her to disagree.

'It is. Look out of the window and you'll see.' Sarah hid her smile, seeing the little girl begin to pout. At least she wasn't still upset after her disturbed night. It was almost as though it had never happened.

She cut toast into fingers and put them on a plate for Emily to eat as soon as she had finished her cereal. 'If it stops raining later on, and things dry out a bit, then we might be able to go,' she conceded. 'If you like, we could make some play dough instead.'

'Yes.' Emily clapped her hands together. 'I like play dough. Can we have the shapes?'

'Yes, I'll find them for you. Which ones do you want—

the stars, circles and squares, or the animals and people shapes?'

Emily made a wide circle with her arms. 'All of them,' she said.

Sarah laughed. 'All of them it is, then.'

A couple of hours later, she looked out of the window at the falling rain. Other parts of the country weren't doing too well as far as the rain was concerned. On the news, there had been talk of flooding in some areas, and she knew that rescue services were being called out to help people who were in trouble.

This was the weekend, though, and she, at least, was enjoying a day off, but that might not be the same for Ben. Would he be at home today?

'I show Ben what I done?' Emily asked, echoing Sarah's thoughts in an uncanny way.

'I don't know if he's at home,' Sarah said. 'He might be working.'

'We go and see.' Emily slid down from her chair at the table, leaving a trail of flour in her wake. She tugged at Sarah's jeans. 'Come on, Mummy. We go and see Ben.'

'Not with those messy hands, we won't.' Sarah frowned, debating whether or not she ought to go and pay him a visit. Common sense told her that she should stay away because whenever she was near to him she found that she was drawn to him more and more. Her emotions were in chaos where he was concerned, and it was difficult enough working with him, let alone seeing him outside work.

It would be all too easy to get involved with him, but surely that would be playing with fire? How did she know whether or not she was free to be with him? How would she cope if she succumbed to her feelings for him and then someone else in her previous life turned up to say that they were man and wife?

Then again, Ben was her neighbour, and it was natural for neighbours to drop by one another's houses, wasn't it? How much harm could it do to pay him a visit? Besides, hadn't she made that last batch of flapjacks with him in mind?

'We'll go and see if he's at home,' she told Emily, 'but you mustn't get upset if he's had to go out.' She paused. 'And we had better clean you up a bit before we go anywhere.'

A few minutes later, she was knocking on Ben's door, huddling under his porch with Emily in order to escape from the worst of the downpour.

'You look like a pair of drowned rats,' Ben said, opening the door. 'Come on in.'

'I wasn't sure whether or not you would have to go to work today,' Sarah said, stepping into the hallway. She shrugged off her jacket and then freed Emily from her plastic raincoat. Ben took the garments from them and hung them up in a small cloakroom to dry. 'Emily wanted to bring you a present,' Sarah told him. 'She made it herself this morning.'

'Did you?' Ben looked at Emily with wide eyes. 'I'm honoured.'

'I maked it, and Mummy put it in the oven, and then I painted it,' Emily said. 'It's a bird and a star.'

By now they were in Ben's large kitchen, and Ben opened up the treasure that had been carefully wrapped up for him in kitchen towel. 'It's a beautiful orange bird,' he said in wonder. 'Is that your favourite colour?'

Emily nodded vigorously. 'The star has lots of colours.' She held the dough creations aloft. 'See? Bird's flying up to the star.'

'So he is. These are lovely. Thank you for that, Emily.' He crouched down to her level and gave her a hug. 'I shall put them on my special shelf, where I shall be able to see them every day.'

Emily gave him a big smile.

'My offering is nothing by comparison,' Sarah said, handing him the tin of flapjacks. 'I made too many, and I remembered that you liked them.'

'You've been trying out the Aga again, haven't you?' He grinned. 'Thank you. We'll have some now, shall we, with a hot drink?'

Emily nodded. 'Flapjacks is yummy,' she said. 'Mummy maked them 'cos I telled her.'

'Oh, well, then, I should say thank you to you as well, shouldn't I?'

Emily returned his smile, but she obviously had other things on her mind. 'Can I play with the little horse and the wishing well in there?' She pointed to a room that Ben used as a study. It could be seen easily through the glass door that opened into it from the hall.

Sarah had seen the room when she'd come to visit briefly with Emily on another occasion, when a ball the little girl had been playing with had gone over into his garden.

There was a polished golden oak desk in the study, with matching filing cabinets, along with bookshelves and a bureau, and in one part of the room Ben had set out model sailing ships and various nautical items. He had a ship's sextant made of brass, along with a ship's compass, both of them polished to a gleaming finish. On another shelf there were a number of small brass ornaments that had caught Emily's attention.

'Yes, I'll get them down for you.' He gave her a smile. 'I expect you want to turn the handle and lift the bucket out of the well, don't you?'

'Yes, and the horse can drink from the bucket.'

Sarah's eyes widened. 'Are you quite sure you know what you're doing?' she asked Ben in a low voice as he walked into the room and started to reach for the ornaments. 'Didn't you tell me that some of the things in here are prized possessions, handed down in the family? As far as I know, Emily's less than three years old, and you're taking a big risk letting her play with them.'

'She can't do much harm, and the model ships and navigation equipment are out of reach. Of course the sextant and ship's compass are definitely items to treasure. My ancestors have something of a tradition of sailing on the high seas.'

She looked at him curiously. 'Did you never feel that you wanted to follow in their footsteps?'

'I can't say that I ever did, although one of my ancestors was a ship's surgeon, so I suppose there's a bit of a connection there. For myself, I've always preferred to keep my feet firmly on dry land.' He handed the ornaments down to Emily, who sat down contentedly on the carpet and began to fill her world with horses and imaginary people.

'I was wondering about that,' Sarah said. 'The dry land, I mean. Only when I was listening to the local news this morning they were saying that the floods are causing problems for people not too far away from here, and I didn't know whether you would be called out. I know some people have to be evacuated from their houses, and there were reports of some elderly residents who were housebound and needing medical attention.'

'It's possible. I suppose there might be a call for the cave rescue team to go out if there are floods underground, and I'm on call with them today. People usually avoid going down into the caves when the weather reports are bad but, you never know, under conditions like these, the rescuers will need all the help they can get. I suppose it's possible that potholers could go underground in dry conditions and meet up with the overflow from a subterranean stream.' He glanced at her briefly. 'Don't look so alarmed. I won't ask you to go with me. I know that you have to take care of Emily.'

Sarah made a face. 'It isn't just that. I don't think I like being near water.' She gave a faint shudder. 'I have a bad feeling about it whenever I see huge flood plains.'

He gave her an assessing look. 'You said the same about caves until you went down there. Anyway, no one likes being caught up in a flood situation.'

He led her towards the kitchen. 'I'll make some tea, and we can keep an eye on Emily through the glass doors.'

'OK.' She smiled. 'Though I expect she'll come running in soon enough when she hears the flapjack tin being opened.'

His kitchen was larger than any she had seen, but it was separated into different areas by clever use of an island cupboard unit and a breakfast bar. All the units were made of wood, finished in a soft eau de nil colour, with glass fronts that allowed for displays of crockery and glassware. The floor was beautifully finished with ceramic tiles that contrasted warmly with the pale colour scheme.

Everything was clean and inviting, and when he showed her to a seat in the dining area at one end of the kitchen, she discovered that she could look out over part of the garden through wide French doors.

'Have you had any more flashbacks?' he asked, pushing a mug of tea in her direction.

'Nothing major,' she said. 'A few isolated pictures of family life, but nothing that gives me any clue as to who I am. I'm beginning to think I might originally have come from hereabouts, though, because some of the places we've passed through on the calls we've attended have seemed vaguely familiar to me—so perhaps that was what my journey here was all about.'

'Coming back to your roots, you mean?'

'Something like that.'

His expression was serious. 'Have you had any more thoughts about who Emily's father might be?'

'No, I haven't. Emily seems to remember him. She doesn't talk about him very much, and when she does, it's usually something like, "Daddy tucked me up in bed," or, "Daddy gived me teddy bear." ' She sighed. 'I keep hoping that a picture of him will come into my mind, or that I'll remember where I was living before I moved here.'

Ben was silent for a moment, his mouth taking on a sombre line, but she couldn't tell what he was thinking. Then he said, 'You'll have to go on being patient. Small things are coming back to you, and that's a really good sign.' He frowned, and studied her for a while longer. 'The head injury was probably enough to cause profound memory loss initially, but it may be that something happened before the injury that made you want to blot out the past.'

'So you're saying that it's psychological?'

'In part, possibly. Added to that, it can't have helped that you came to live in a different area from where you had been living before, because it means that you have none of the associations that other people in similar circumstances would have been able to rely on.'

Sarah braced herself to ask the question that was worrying her most of all. 'Do you think there's a cut-off point where my memory would never return?'

He shook his head. 'The fact that you lost your memory for several months would usually mean that it wasn't likely that you would recover, but given that you've had some instances of flashback, and that there might have been some psychological trauma to contend with, I'd say you could still hope to recall a good deal of what went before.'

She was quiet for a moment, absorbing that. Finally, she said, 'That's good…I think.' What could have happened that had been so bad she didn't want to go back there in her mind?

He ran a hand lightly down her arm in a gesture of compassion. 'You're strong, Sarah, and you have a remarkable sense of self-preservation. You've shown tremendous spirit, pushing yourself to take on new challenges, and you've even managed to make a happy home for Emily, despite what she must have been through, so you have to take some comfort from that. You're one of life's survivors.'

He would have said more, but his phone began to ring, and he moved away from her to go and answer it. From his expression, she could see that it was not good news.

'I have to go out,' he said, coming back to her after he had cut the call. 'It's as I said. It appears that some people are late returning from a caving expedition, and there's a chance that their exit might have been cut off underground. We have to go and try to get them out before the water level rises too far.'

He looked tense at the prospect and Sarah felt for him and for the plight of the cavers.

'You won't take any risks, will you? I mean, you'll make sure that you always have a clear way out?' Anxiety shimmered through her.

'Of course.' He smiled, aiming to reassure her, but she knew it wouldn't be as simple as that.

'Please, be careful,' she said. What would she do if anything bad happened to him? She couldn't bear the thought.

'I will.'

He went to get ready, and Sarah gathered up Emily and told her that it was time for them to go home. Part of her wanted to go with him, but part of her felt a dread and frustration at the thought of being pinned down and overwhelmed by fast-flowing water. She couldn't explain it, even to herself, but the fear was there, gnawing at her.

Throughout the rest of the day she fretted, waiting to hear the sound of Ben's car returning, and she watched the local news intently whenever there was a snippet to be had on television.

By early evening, he still hadn't returned, and Sarah's nerves were reaching crisis point. Was there some way she could go in search of him? But Carol was away, and she didn't know anyone who she could call on to babysit.

Defeated, she contemplated putting Emily to bed, but just as she was about to gather her up for her evening bath, her phone rang.

She knew a quick sense of relief. Was Ben calling her to say that he was on his way home?

It wasn't Ben on the line, though, and Sarah's spirits plummeted. It was Jennifer who was calling, and she sounded anxious.

'Sarah, I'm sorry to bother you, but I'm worried about Ben. He rang me earlier to say that he might not be able to come round, that he had to go out. He said he would let me know when he was home, but I've heard nothing. Do you know if he's back yet?'

'I'm sorry. I haven't heard from him either, Jennifer. It might be that the rescue is taking longer than they expected, especially if someone is injured.'

'That's just it,' Jennifer said. 'I know that those people were brought out some time ago, because I have a friend whose nephew was one of those who were trapped, and she rang me to tell me. They're being transported to hospital now, but most of the roads thereabouts are flooded.'

'Perhaps he stopped off somewhere to relax for an hour or so on the way home. He could be with friends.'

'Then he would have called me. I can't help feeling that something's wrong. I've been listening to the news on the radio, and they're saying all sorts of things about floods in the region where Ben might be. There's talk of cars being swept away, and people being trapped. I'm really worried that something might have happened to him.'

Sarah could understand her concern. She had been thinking the very same thing. 'I wish I could go and see for myself what's happening, maybe even lend a hand, but I have Emily with me, and I can't take her over to Carol's house because she's gone to visit relatives for the weekend.'

'You could bring her over to me, if you like. I'll look after her for you…as long as you promise me you won't get yourself into any danger. All you would need to do would be to ask the emergency service people if they know anything.'

'Yes, but you're not well enough to take on the burden,'

Sarah said. 'I could see for myself the other day that your breathing is still not right.'

'I'm really very much better,' Jennifer told her. 'Besides, I expect Emily will be about ready to settle down for the night, won't she? I have a bed in the guest room where she could sleep, and I'm sure she'll be fine if you bring some of her toys along with her.'

Sarah's mind raced as she thought it through. It was true that Emily was sleepy, and if she were to leave her for just an hour or two, Jennifer wouldn't come to any great harm through looking after her, would she?

'All right, if you're sure that you will be able to manage,' she said.

'I'm sure.'

Emily thought it was a great adventure to be going along to Jennifer's house. 'See Nana Jenny?' she said, and Sarah felt a brief tug at her insides at the innocent reference.

'Yes,' she murmured, 'but you must promise me that you'll be good for Jenny. She's been poorly.'

'I be good,' Emily said solemnly. Then she smiled. 'She give me biscuits, and I play with her dollies.'

Sarah left her in Jennifer's care some half an hour later, and drove to the place where she thought Ben was most likely to be.

None of the emergency service personnel who were still directing operations near to the cave rescue site had any idea where he might be. 'You say he was wearing a medic's outfit?' a policeman said.

Sarah nodded. 'He went out with the cave rescue team.'

'They've all gone by now,' the officer said. 'We're just here to post warning signs in place. The last I saw of them, they were headed back to where the cars were parked, over on the rise. If he came in his own car, and not in the rescue van, then that's where he would have been.'

'Yes, he did.' She had phoned the leader of the rescue team before she'd set out, and he'd assured her that Ben had begun to make his own way home. But that had been some time ago.

Sarah looked where the officer indicated. The parking area was situated well clear of the floods, and she guessed that the road up there would lead them away from any danger areas.

'I'll go and take a closer look,' she murmured.

She went back to her car and drove towards the higher level, but when she reached the parking area, she could see that Ben's car wasn't there.

What could have happened to him? She rummaged in the glove compartment for her map, and checked the routes that he might have taken. Was it possible that he would have inadvertently chosen to return via a road that was under floodwater? Surely that must have been the case, or why wasn't he home already?

Sarah was becoming more concerned as time went by. He might not have thought to ring her and let her know where he was, but he would have given Jennifer a call, if only to stop her from worrying.

She put the map away and began to drive off in the direction that she thought Ben might have taken. There was meadowland on either side, and the river cut through the hills some distance away.

Some twenty minutes or so later, she realised that things were beginning to look really bad. The river was closer to the road now, and she could see that there was a bridge spanning it at one point, but the water level had almost reached the highest point of the bridge.

Up ahead, the river had burst its banks and water spilled out over the road. Debris floated on its surface, branches, leaves, and straw from the fields. Cars had been abandoned, and some further along the road were beginning to shift as the torrent tried to carry them with it. She came across a rescue vehicle, set back on dry ground, clear of the flood plain, and she decided to park her car behind it. Then she stepped out and went to investigate.

It was raining once more, and the droplets lashed at her, stinging her face and causing her hair to curl into damp tendrils. She was wearing a pair of knee-length boots that she hoped might serve to keep out some of the wet, and she pulled her jacket tightly round her, but she soon realised that it wasn't the dampness that she had to fear. It was the sheer force of the water that pounded her legs that gave her most cause for concern as she tried to wade through the turbulent stream. Added to that, the noise of the raging river was frightening, a deafening sound, like a high wind storming through the trees.

She hoped that nobody was in the cars, but as she approached, she saw that there were men wearing luminous jackets deployed at various points along the flooded road. They appeared to be helping people, moving them back towards drier ground.

'Is there anything I can do to help?' she asked, stopping alongside a couple of the rescue workers. They were carrying an elderly lady between them, clasping their hands together in a kind of cradle, aiming to keep her above the water.

The older man shook his head. 'It's best if you stay out of harm's way,' he said. 'Leave it to us.'

'Are people trapped in their cars?' she asked.

He nodded, and then moved on. Sarah kept on going to the place they had come from, peering into the cars that she came across. In one, a little girl, around six years old, was crying, huddled in the back of a vehicle next to her mother. Sarah tried to open the door to get to them. She guessed the mother had gone into the back seat to comfort her child.

The door wouldn't move. 'Try pushing from your side,' she shouted to the woman, but even though they both tried their best, the door wouldn't budge. 'Can you wind the window down?'

The woman tried the handle, but then shook her head. 'It won't move.'

'What about the sunroof? If you can open that, you can pass the little girl out through the sunroof to me.'

The woman was shaking, but she did as Sarah had suggested, and after a moment or two Sarah was reaching up to hold the little girl safe in her arms. 'I'll take her to the rescue vehicle and come back for you,' Sarah told the mother.

The mother nodded, but just then the car seemed to lift and sway, and the woman sent Sarah a petrified look. Sarah thought that she looked ill, but perhaps it was just that terror had made her feel faint.

'I'll come back for you, I promise,' Sarah said again.

Wading through the swirling water, she made her way back the way she had come. By now an ambulance had arrived, and the old lady was sitting inside it, being tended to. Sarah handed over the little girl into the care of the paramedics and then started back towards the girl's mother.

Catching up with one of the rescue workers, she told him about the woman in the car, pointing out the vehicle through the lashing rain. 'The car's beginning to move with the force of the water,' she told him, as she waded beside him through the flood water. 'She must be terrified.'

'Yes, I imagine she is.' He winced, and she guessed he was trying to prioritise the situation. 'The trouble is, a number of people were caught unawares, and it's taking time for us to get to them all. We've called for more people to come and help.'

He frowned. 'The doctor's working up ahead. If he's finished attending to his patient, I'll see if we can rope him in to help out.'

'You have a doctor here?' She shot the man a quick, alert glance. 'Do you happen to know his name? It's just that I'm looking for someone—he's a doctor working with the cave rescue team.'

Suddenly she swayed with the pressure of the water and toppled over. A moment of sheer panic rippled through her, but then the man by her side reached out and grabbed her arm, lifting her clear of the icy water.

'Thanks,' she said, gasping and trying to catch her breath. She could see that he, too, was battling against the current.

'This would probably be your man.' The rescue worker pointed up ahead, and Sarah saw that someone was approaching the woman's car. 'It looks as though he's finished with his patient. That's him, going over to the car.'

Sarah felt a rush of relief surge through her when she saw that it really was Ben. He was using all his strength to divert the movement of the car, trying to push it towards the trunk of a huge tree, and she guessed that he was hoping the tree would act as a buttress.

'Thank heaven,' she muttered under her breath. A warm

feeling wrapped itself around her heart. Was this love that she felt for him, this overwhelming feeling of joy that swept over her now that she had found him? 'He's safe.'

They both went to help him, and between them they managed to steady the car and stop its sideways motion. Ben glanced at her, a look of shock passing over his features, and she guessed he was alarmed by her wet state. 'What are you doing here?' he asked, his tone curt. Then, 'No, don't answer that. Let's try to get the door open. We need to get this woman out of here.'

Together they worked on the door, and in a minute or two they were able to reach inside to lift the woman out. Sarah could see that she was in a bad way. Her breathing was coming in short gasps, and her head lolled back as though she was faint.

Ben and the rescue worker carried her back towards the dry ground, and Sarah found herself struggling to stay upright as she went with them.

'Hold onto my jacket,' Ben said in a taut voice. 'The last thing we need is for you to get swept away.'

Back at the ambulance, Ben settled the woman into a seat and started to examine her.

'Her blood pressure's way off the scale,' he said. 'It looks as though she's going through a hypertensive crisis.'

'That's bad, isn't it?' Sarah whispered, aware that the little girl was near tears at seeing her mother in this state. She gave the girl a reassuring hug.

'It's not good.' He opened up a medical case and started to draw up medication into a syringe. 'This will help to calm things until we can get her to hospital,' he said.

It took a while for the injection to work, but he stayed with the woman until she appeared to be breathing more normally and then nodded to the ambulance driver to say that it was all right to start the engine.

He stepped down from the ambulance, leaving the people inside to the care of the paramedics, and reached up to help Sarah down onto the road.

The ambulance moved away, and Ben's gaze flicked over her, his expression tense. 'What on earth are you doing here?' he asked. 'You haven't brought Emily out in this weather, have you?'

'No, of course not.' Sarah pulled in a ragged breath. 'She's with your mother.'

He frowned. 'I've already said that my mother isn't well enough to look after Emily. Why would you leave her to cope with a small child?'

'We were worried about you,' Sarah said, alarmed by his terse reaction. 'We thought something might have happened to stop you from getting home.'

'Well, you were right about that, but it wasn't anything that needed to bring you out here.'

Sarah took a step backwards, uncertain about his mood. 'I'm sorry if you feel that way.' A shiver ran through her. Now that she was back on firm ground, it was beginning to dawn on her that the whole experience of being out here had been horrifying. She was soaked through to the skin, her body was clammy with cold, and Ben was angry with her.

Why was he acting this way? Why had she ever thought that she loved him, or that he might in some small way care for her?

But the truth was, no matter how foolish it might be, no matter that she should have known better, she had lost her heart to him, but he didn't seem to care about that. He was throwing her feelings back in her face.

She blinked, trying to brush away the tears that pricked her eyes, and she pressed her lips together to stop them from trembling. She would not cry. She wouldn't.

CHAPTER EIGHT

'I DON'T understand what could have possessed you to come out here,' Ben said, a cutting edge to his voice. 'You were perfectly safe at home, but look at you now. You're wet through, shivering with cold, and all for nothing.' He glowered at her. 'I thought you told me that you had a bad feeling about being near stretches of water? So why put yourself through something like this?'

'I've already tried to explain,' Sarah answered in an equally taut manner, spoiled only by the fact that her teeth were chattering. 'I don't much care whether you approve or not.' She returned his glare. 'I'm going back to my car.' Before she started off in that direction, though, she threw him one last look. 'You should phone your mother. She's worried sick about you.'

'Sarah, you can't just walk off like that,' he said, coming after her and stopping her in her tracks. 'For one thing, you'll catch your death of cold, and for another, you might run into difficulties. You don't know which of these roads is passable.'

'And you do? How is it that you ended up here, then?'

'I had a call from the rescue services to say that a man was having a heart attack. They had just pulled him from his car.

I expect it was the sight of the river bursting its banks that sent him into shock.'

'Oh.' Sarah's response was subdued, her voice small as all the fight went out of her. She felt thoroughly miserable, and now her whole body was racked with shivers. 'Is he all right?'

'He should be. I managed to get to him in time.' He frowned. 'We should get you into the rescue vehicle,' he said. 'They have blankets in there and flasks of hot chocolate. We need to get you warmed up before the cold makes you ill.'

She was tempted to ignore his suggestion, given that he had been so offhand with her, but the thought of hot chocolate and blankets undermined her resolve. She turned towards the vehicle.

'You should take off your wet clothes and wrap yourself in these,' Ben said, handing her a couple of blankets once she was safely inside the roomy van. There was no one else around, and she guessed the men were still helping the stranded motorists.

'I can't do that,' she murmured. 'I still have to drive myself home.'

He shook his head. 'I'll take you in my car. We can come back tomorrow and fetch yours.' He studied her briefly. 'I'll stand guard outside the van while you change, and when you're ready I'll move your car to a place where it will be out of reach of the floodwater. Do you want to pass me your keys?'

Reluctantly, she reached into her jacket pocket and re-trieved them. He was taking over, and she was too drained to put up any more of a fight, so she handed them to him and waited while he climbed out of the van and closed the doors behind him.

A few minutes later, he was rapping on the metal. 'Are you ready for me to come in?'

'Yes,' she said. She was as ready as she would ever be. This whole episode was turning out to be a disaster.

He opened the doors once more and climbed in beside her. 'Would you like some hot chocolate?' he asked.

She nodded, and waited while he unscrewed the cap from the flask and poured the hot liquid into a cup.

'Here you are,' he said, holding out the cup to her and gently pressing her hands around it. He didn't let go but supported the cup, and she guessed that he must realise that her hands were trembling so much she might drop it. 'I don't know how hot it is, so be careful. Sip it slowly.'

He sat beside her on the bench seat in the van, and waited until she had finished drinking. Then he took the cup from her and put it to one side.

She stared around her in a disconsolate fashion, feeling warmer inside, but still there was this chill of isolation that surrounded her.

He slid an arm around her, drawing her against the warmth of his body. 'What am I going to do with you?' he said on a heavy sigh. 'I can't leave you to your own devices, because I never know when you're going to land yourself in trouble of some sort.'

'I would have managed perfectly well,' she said, her tone grumpy. 'Anyone could have fallen over in those conditions.'

'That's exactly what I mean,' he said. 'The whole point is, you didn't have to be here.' He shook his head. 'If you're not getting stuck climbing into people's houses, or nearly drowning yourself in floodwater, it's that you're quite likely to take it into your head to do something beyond your capabilities—like moving house when you could have stayed with Carol.'

'I thought you understood about that,' she said, giving him an accusing stare. 'Anyway, it worked out just fine.'

'It did, but it might just as easily have gone wrong.'

'Why should that worry you?' she muttered in a tight voice. 'You're not my keeper.'

'Maybe not, but I feel responsible. I feel that I need to watch over you...you and Emily.'

Sarah straightened up and pushed her damp hair from her forehead, twisting the unruly locks behind her ear. 'You don't have to feel that way,' she said, pride stiffening her back. 'There are enough people looking out for Emily, with Carol and the health visitors and Social Services. If anything happens to me, she'll be well looked after.'

He drew her close to him, wrapping both arms around her. 'I didn't mean it in that way. I worry about you. I don't want anything to happen to you.'

She looked up at him, and his gaze was moving over her, drinking in every part of her face—her forehead, her temples, the straight line of her nose, and the slope of her cheekbones. Then his glance shifted to the soft, full curve of her mouth, and he started to move towards her, lowering his head, his eyes darkening to a smoky blue grey.

He was going to kiss her, she knew it, she could feel it in every fibre of her being, and her body began to tingle in awareness, heat sweeping through her as she anticipated that heart-stopping moment.

But then he seemed to think better of it and he became still for a moment or two, before easing back from her.

Disappointment washed through her.

'We should get you home,' he said in a roughened voice. 'You need to get into some warm, dry clothes.'

She nodded, swallowing hard. She didn't have it in her to argue with him any more, and the thought of driving herself home filled her with dismay.

He told her that he would drop her off at the cottage, and when she demurred and said that she wanted to go and collect Emily he said, 'I've already spoken to my mother about that. She says that Emily is tucked up in bed, fast asleep. It would be a shame to disturb her.'

'But what if she has a nightmare and wakes up?'

'I'll be there to talk to her. I'm going to stay over at my mother's house, to keep an eye on both of them. I'll be sleeping on the sofa, so you have no need to worry.'

'But I will worry.' A steely glint came into her eyes. 'I know that your mother doesn't have a spare bed, but I could sleep in a chair in Emily's room, couldn't I?'

He began to chuckle. 'My mother said that you would say that.' He nodded, and held his hands up in a gesture of defeat. 'OK, you win. We'll do whatever you want.'

He dropped Sarah off at his mother's house, and while she was talking to Jennifer he slipped away, saying that he had to go and collect something. Sarah frowned, wondering what it was that could be so important.

Some half an hour later he returned, and he had with him a put-you-up bed, along with a duvet and pillows. 'I'll set this up in Emily's room,' he said.

She went with him, anxious that he shouldn't disturb the little girl. Jennifer had lent her a bathrobe, and now she pulled it more securely around her, tying the sash firmly.

'That was thoughtful of you,' she said in a low voice.

'Well, I think you need a good night's sleep,' he murmured, 'after your drenching today.' He looked her over. 'How are you feeling? Are you going to be all right? I'd hate to think that both of you were going to be having nightmares.'

'I'll be fine, thanks. It was a scary feeling, being out there near the river, as it was getting dark, especially when I went in the water. I thought I was going to give way to panic. I don't know why I should feel that way. It's something I can't explain, but it isn't a physical fear, it's more an association that I can't place. I do sometimes have bad dreams, but I don't understand them, and I just hope that my subconscious will work it all out for me.'

'There could be something in that,' he agreed. He sent a quick look around the room. 'If you need anything in the night, if you're upset, or need to talk, I'll be just downstairs in the living room.'

She nodded. 'Thanks.' She didn't for a moment intend to call on him, but just the knowledge that he had offered was enough to warm her heart.

Fortunately, Emily slept through the night without waking, and in the morning she was her usual lively self, eager to be off to nursery where she could play with her friends.

'I play in the home corner today,' she told everybody. 'I make the dinner on the cooker, and then I put the cups out and pour tea for everyone.' She looked as though the prospect was a blissful one.

'Isn't it lovely to have the innocence of childhood?' Jennifer said, looking on with amusement. 'It must be good for you to know that she's contented while you're working,' she added, glancing at Sarah.

'It is.' She squeezed Jennifer's hand lightly before starting to clear away the breakfast dishes. 'Thank you for looking after her so well last night.'

'It was wonderful to have her here.' Jennifer stood up and began to take crockery over to the dishwasher. 'Are you sure that you feel up to going to work today? I'm sure that Ben would explain to the others if you feel that you need to take some time off. It must have been a shocking experience, to be carried off your feet by the water that way.'

Sarah shook her head. 'No, it's not necessary. I can manage perfectly well. In fact, I look forward to going out with the ambulance team. I suppose it takes me out of myself and keeps me busy and alert.'

'That's good,' Ben said, looking at his watch. 'If you're sure you're up to it, we should be getting ready to go in the next few minutes.'

She was still going out with him in the rapid-response car, rather than travelling with the ambulance, and they made several calls that morning to people who had been involved in various kinds of accidents, from falling off a horse to slipping down a rocky crag.

It was a joy to watch Ben at work. He was good at his job, and he had an easy manner with the patients, soothing their anxieties or cheering them up with his light banter.

In the afternoon, while they were with the paramedics, attending to casualties of a road traffic accident, Ben took another call. He listened carefully, and then frowned. 'Yes, we should be able to manage that. It's only about a mile away from here.'

A moment later, he ended the call and spoke to one of the paramedics. 'Will you be able to cope here if Sarah and I go off to another incident?' he asked. 'It's at the school, just a short distance away from here.'

The paramedic nodded. 'We're about finished here. We'll come to you as soon as we're free.'

Ben began to walk back to the car. 'Where are we going?' Sarah asked.

'It's a school sports field just five minutes away,' he told her. 'A boy has suffered an ankle injury while he was playing football.'

They slid inside the car, and he started off in the direction of the school. 'It's on our way back to the hospital, so it wouldn't be worth calling out another ambulance.'

When they arrived at the sports field, boys were milling around the injured lad, trying to see what had happened. As soon as Ben and Sarah arrived, the teacher sent the class back to the field to go on with the game. 'Alex will be well taken care of,' he said. 'Let the doctor do his job in peace. I want you boys to be ready for the match this weekend. Go on with the game. Mr Jones will take over from me to supervise you.'

Once some space had been cleared around the boy, Ben knelt down to examine him.

'That must have been some tackle,' he said, looking at the area of bruising and swelling around the ankle. 'I think you've actually broken a bone. I wonder what happened to the boy you clashed with?'

'I think he's all right,' the boy said, gritting his teeth to fight the pain. 'He was winded, and he went to sit down.' Alex was about fourteen years old and sturdily built.

The boy's teacher was worried. 'I've called his parents. They're on their way.'

'That's good.' Ben glanced at the boy, who was squeezing

his eyelids together in an attempt to hold back tears. 'I'm going to give you something to ease the pain and then we'll put a splint around the ankle so that it doesn't move. After that, we'll get you into the ambulance and take you to hospital.'

He looked at Sarah. 'Would you get me the splints from the car while I give him a painkiller?'

'Yes, of course.' She hurried back to the car and rummaged in the boot for the splints. Walking back towards the injured boy, she glanced around and saw that his classmates were running about the field once more…all except for one, who was sitting down alone, leaning back against the wire fence. He didn't look too well, and she wondered if he was the boy who had tackled Alex.

She put the splints down on the grass beside Ben. 'Would it be all right if I go and look at the boy over there?' she murmured. 'He doesn't look too well, and I could perhaps talk to him and make sure that everything's OK.'

Ben glanced over to where the boy was sitting. 'Yes, that's OK. I'll be a few minutes here yet. I want to make sure that the injection works before I attempt to immobilise the ankle.'

Sarah went over to the boy, who was sitting quite close to where the rapid-response car was parked. She said softly, 'Were you hurt at all in the game?'

'I…don't…think so.' He struggled to get the words out. 'The teacher told me to…sit here.'

Sarah looked at him worriedly. He was a tall, lean boy, and his face looked ashen. His lips had a bluish tinge about them, and she found herself thinking that this was more than a simple case of exhaustion. 'What's your name?' she asked.

'Matthew.'

'You don't look too well, Matthew,' she said. 'I could get the doctor to come and have a look at you as soon as he's finished with Alex's ankle.'

The boy didn't answer but suddenly slumped over onto the grass. Alarmed, Sarah felt for a pulse but couldn't find one. Then she realised that he wasn't breathing. She called out for help and started chest compressions and mouth-to-mouth re-suscitation, but her efforts seemed to be getting her nowhere, and it suddenly occurred to her that both the oxygen and defibrillator were in the car.

'Can I do something to help?' The boy's teacher suddenly appeared by her side.

'Yes, go on with the chest compressions and the mouth-to-mouth resuscitation while I go and get the defibrillator.' She checked to make sure that he knew what he was doing, then went and reached into the boot of the car and pulled out the machine, along with the ventilation equipment.

Just a few seconds later she had attached the bag device to the oxygen mask and put it in place over the boy's airway. Then she instructed the teacher how to press down on the bag so that the oxygen was pumped into the child's lungs. 'See how his chest is rising and falling?' she asked.

He nodded.

'OK, keep on doing that, and make sure that the air keeps going in where it's supposed to.'

She checked Matthew's pulse once more, and was dismayed by her findings. She switched on the defibrillator and began to open up his shirt so that she could attach the elec-trode pads to the boy's chest.

'Stand clear,' she told the teacher. The automatic defibrillator assessed the boy's heart rhythm, and then delivered a shock to the heart.

'Keep on with the ventilation,' Sarah said, beginning chest compressions once more.

'He has a pulse now,' Ben said, coming to kneel by her side, a moment later. 'He's beginning to breathe by himself.'

Sarah looked up at him. How long had he been there?

Perhaps he'd read her thoughts, because he said, 'I've only just arrived. I heard you shout, and as soon as I could I came to see what was happening. I didn't realise that you were using the defibrillator until it was too late.'

'I knew what to do.'

He gave her a strange, assessing look. 'So it seems. Anyway, the ambulance has just arrived.'

'Good. We need to get him on board.' Sarah frowned. 'The sooner he's in hospital, the better. It's unusual for a boy this age to have heart problems like this, but I think he should be checked over for problems of arrhythmia. There might even be a history of such problems within the family.'

Ben looked at her oddly. 'What kind of treatment would help in that situation?' he asked casually.

'That would depend on the type of arrhythmia. Possibly he would be started on beta-blocker therapy, but if his condition didn't improve, he might need to have an implant to prevent any further attacks. It all depends what the tests reveal.' She glanced at the heart monitor. 'At the moment he has a sinus rhythm with premature ventricular beats.' She looked up at Ben. 'He's having problems with his breathing, and I think it would be wise to intubate him so that he has a secure airway in place while he's being monitored.'

'I think you're right,' he said. 'I'll do it before we put him in the ambulance.' He studied her as he started to pull the equipment out of the boot of the car. 'Do you realise what you've just done?'

She stared at him. 'What do you mean? I was trying to help him. Are you saying that I did the wrong thing?'

'Not at all.' He didn't take his eyes off her as he walked back to the patient. 'I'm saying that you did what any doctor would have done. I don't think you know all these things that you write about purely by chance—I think you must have trained as a doctor at some time. You acted on instinct, and you saved his life.'

Strangely, Sarah felt as though she had been punched in the chest. Her lungs were suddenly desperate for air, and her heart was beginning to pound. All the time she had been tending to the boy she had been working purely on instinct, not thinking, not worrying whether she was doing the right thing, but it had all seemed perfectly natural, as though she had the skills at her fingertips. It hadn't occurred to her that none of this was normal.

By now the teacher was looking at them both as though he was confused by what was going on.

'It's all right,' Ben told him. 'I'll take over from you now. Perhaps you could go and call his parents. We'll be taking him to hospital for observation.'

The teacher got to his feet, looking back at them as he started to walk away. Ben put a tube in place in the boy's throat and attached the oxygen device.

'He'll need to go to an intensive care unit. I expect they'll start him on an infusion for the arrhythmia, and they'll do an echocardiogram to see what's going on with the heart.'

Sarah stood up, feeling a little shaky. 'You're not angry with me, then?'

Ben gave her an amused look. 'Angry? Far from it. What we need to do now, though, is find out where you did your training and see if we can figure out how much you do know.'

'Perhaps that's all there is.' Sarah frowned. She was having trouble taking any of this in, and the fact that Ben was accepting it as though nothing was wrong made her more confused than ever.

He shook his head. 'I don't believe it, not for a second. One thing I do know is that your memory is coming back to you, piece by piece.'

The paramedics came over to them. 'We've put the boy with the ankle fracture into the ambulance. Is this another patient for us?'

'Yes, he is. Let's get him to hospital as soon as we can.'

They followed the ambulance in the fast-response car, and Sarah was anxious all the time, concerned about the young boy. She fidgeted in her seat and wished that the miles could be swallowed up in one big gulp.

'Do your parents work in medicine?' Ben asked, throwing her an interested glance. 'Sometimes it follows that a doctor's son or daughter will follow in his or her footsteps.'

Sarah shook her head. 'My father works for a pharmaceutical company. He had to go and work overseas to supervise a new development out there. My mother was working, too. They went together.'

Then, as she realised what she had said, she clapped a hand over her mouth. 'How do I know that?' She turned to Ben and looked at him, her expression shocked. 'You did that on purpose, didn't you? You asked me, as though I would come up with the answer without even thinking about it.'

'And that's exactly what you did.'

'Yes.' Sarah was shaking inside. Instead of feeling over-joyed at the memories that were coming back, she felt a well of fear and dread building up inside her. What was wrong with her?

'What's happening to me, Ben?' she asked, and there was a noticeable tremor in her voice. 'I'm so scared. I don't know if I can face this.'

Ben drove the car into a lay-by and cut the engine. 'It's all right,' he said. 'Come here. Let me hold you.'

He reached for her and she went willingly into his arms and let him soothe away the feelings of apprehension and terror that were threatening to overwhelm her. It should have been a wonderful thing that all these memories were coming back to her, but to Sarah it seemed as though a void was opening up in front of her, a dark place of unknown happen-ings whose revelations could make her whole again or might destroy her.

She gave a soft whimper and buried her face in Ben's shirt front.

'You don't have to face it alone,' he said softly, stroking her silky hair. 'I'm here with you. I promise you I won't let you go through any of this on your own.'

CHAPTER NINE

'DID Emily go off to Carol's house all right this morning?'
Ben was standing by the table in his kitchen, making a last-minute check of the contents of his medical bag. He looked across the room at Sarah.

'Yes, she was as bright and cheery as ever.' She smiled. 'I think Carol was really glad to see her. Her other two foster-children have gone back to their parents, so she's feeling a little bit at a loose end at the moment. She's pleased for the children, of course, because the parents seem to be trying to work things out.'

He pushed his stethoscope into the bag and fastened the clasp. 'She's been good for Emily, hasn't she? And good for you, too, because it means that you can go out to work.'

'I don't know what I would have done without her,' Sarah said. 'As to work, shouldn't I be going out with the ambulance crew today?'

'Under normal circumstances, yes. My colleague is on the rota for going on call with the rapid-response car this month, but he has an appointment this morning so I'll be taking his place until he returns at lunchtime. It means that I'll be able to follow up in A and E this afternoon, and I thought it might be a good idea if you were to come along with me. It might help to spark off one or two recollections if you were to put yourself back in a hospital situation.'

'Because you believe that I'm actually a doctor?'

He nodded. 'That's right. We've no idea whether you specialised in any particular area, or even whether you were a GP, but it can't hurt to go into the unit and get the feel of the place, can it? It might be that the surroundings are different from what you were used to, but the principles are the same wherever you are.'

Sarah mulled that over. 'I suppose that's true, and as far as the job goes and staying with the response car for another day, Admin won't mind how I get my information for the report.'

'True.' Ben went to collect his jacket from the cloakroom and said in a brisk tone, 'Are we ready to go, then?'

Sarah nodded, taking one last glance around the kitchen. 'I love this house,' she said with a soft sigh. 'The rooms are filled with light, and everything is just perfect. It makes me feel tranquil, just being here. You've even managed to landscape the garden so that it looks like a natural part of the Peak District. All those beautiful trees, and the rockery with its mossy stones…it's a haven for wildlife.'

She turned to him and smiled. 'I sometimes look over at your garden from my kitchen window and watch the birds flocking to the birdtable. Emily can even tell you the names of some of them.'

'She's a bright little thing, that one, and she comes out with things quite unexpectedly from time to time.' His gaze flicked over her. 'She mentioned her grandparents once, didn't she? I remember that she was disappointed that she hadn't seen them in a while.'

Sarah pulled in a deep breath to steady herself. 'She seems to have a lot stored away in her mind, but because she's as young as she is it's difficult for her to express herself.'

'Hmm...I wondered if we should work on trying to find your parents. You said that your father worked for a pharmaceutical company, and it shouldn't be too difficult to find out whether a relatively high-profile employee has gone to work abroad. I'm assuming that he must be in a position of authority if he's supervising a new development. There can't be that many international companies, and provided that we explain the situation we might find that the executives are willing to help us out. We'd be more likely to strike lucky if we point out that his daughter has gone missing.'

He studied her for a moment and she guessed he was trying to gauge her reaction. Then he added, 'It occurred to me that Sarah Hall might have been your maiden name. If it was your married name, we would probably have found your true identity by now.'

Sarah frowned. 'But Emily said her name is Hall. Are you saying it's possible that I was never married?'

'That could be so. These things happen, and children are born to single mothers all the time, but at least it gives us a starting point for trying to find your parents.' He stopped as he was about to open the front door and studied her thoughtfully for a second or two. 'Would you like me to see what I can find out?'

'That would be great,' she said, thinking it through. 'I tried to find them myself some time ago, but I kept coming up against dead ends, and I'm not sure that I could face going through the process all over again. It would be good if you were to help...if you don't mind doing that for me?'

'Leave it with me,' he murmured.

They went out to the car, and from then on they concentrated on the job in hand. Sarah spent the morning making notes as Ben and the paramedics tended to their patients.

Around lunchtime they went to a place where a man had been found slumped at the wheel of his car. Luckily, he had pulled over to the side of the road where he wouldn't be a danger to anyone, but someone had called an ambulance because something didn't look right about the way he was sitting there.

'His skin is warm, but his pulse is very faint,' Jamie, one of the paramedics, said. He spoke to the man, but there was no response, and his colleague went to fetch a stretcher.

Ben set about checking the patient's reflexes. 'There's no sign that he suffered a stroke. Are there any substances in the car to suggest that he might have taken something that caused him to collapse?'

Jamie went to look. 'Nothing.'

Sarah checked the heart monitor. 'He has sinus tachycardia, but there's no evidence of a heart attack. Could he be suffering from anaphylactic shock?'

'It's possible,' Ben murmured, preparing to set up an intravenous line. 'Let's give him normal saline and see if that helps to revive him.'

'It doesn't seem to be having much effect,' Jamie remarked a while later.

Ben winced. 'I'll give him an antihistamine and a subcutaneous injection of epinephrine to see if that will do the trick. Whatever happens, we need to get him to A and E right away.'

The man was still unresponsive after the medication, and

Sarah was worried. 'His pulse rate's increasing, but there's still no readable signal on the pulse oximeter, is there?'

'No, but at least he's breathing. We'll give him supplemental oxygen via the mask.' He turned to Jamie. 'Let's get him to hospital.'

Jamie nodded. He was a young man, in his thirties, with neatly cropped dark hair and friendly grey eyes. Sarah followed him into the ambulance, noting down the equipment that had been used and the procedures that had been followed.

'How are those two young lads doing?' Jamie asked, as he checked that the patient's oxygen mask was in place. 'I mean the ones that we looked after on the sports field the other day. Have you heard anything about them since then?'

'Yes, I have,' Sarah told him. 'I rang the hospital to see if I could find out what had happened to them. It turns out that Ben was right when he said Alex must have broken his ankle. It was put in a cast and it's just a question of checking up over the next few weeks to make sure that it's healing OK.'

She helped Jamie to secure the stretcher in place. 'As to Matthew, they've done quite a few tests, and it looks as though he has a condition that means he might at any time suffer dangerous arrhythmia. They've stabilised him for the time being, but they're going to give him an implant that will regulate his heartbeat and stop him from suffering any more nasty episodes.'

Jamie adjusted the position of the saline bag. 'I'm glad that he's all right.' The paramedic gave her an approving look. 'I think you're doing really well in this job. I know that you're only meant to be reporting on the use of the equipment and the difficulties of doing the job, but you've become part of the team.'

Sarah smiled. 'Thanks.' His comment caused a warm glow to surge inside her.

They stepped down from the ambulance, and Jamie was thoughtful for a moment or two as he pushed the ramp back inside the vehicle and shut the doors. 'It must be difficult for you, working in emergency medicine and looking after your little girl. My wife has trouble juggling work and child care, and our children are older than your Emily.'

Sarah gave a faint grimace. 'I'm only working part time. It would be more of a problem if I had to come out every day. At least I can do my reports and some of the newspaper work from home, and I get to be with Emily for a good part of the week.'

'That's true enough.' He smiled and gave a slight wave of his hand as he moved to the front of the vehicle.

A second or two later the ambulance moved off along the road, and Sarah went back to the car with Ben. She was subdued, lost in thought, and it was only when she was settled in the passenger seat beside him and they were on their way to the hospital that Ben said, 'Something's troubling you, isn't it? You've been quiet ever since you spoke to Jamie about the boys.'

She gave a diffident shrug. 'I think it was something he said, about it being difficult for me, working in emergency medicine. It seemed to strike a chord somehow, but I don't have any problems right now, so it must be to do with something from the past.'

'You obviously haven't discovered what it was that bothered you.' His gaze ran over her. 'Perhaps you should just let it be for the moment. Sometimes you can think too hard about a problem, and the answer keeps evading you. Then, when you least expect it, it pops into your head.'

'You mean that I should let my subconscious go to work on it?' She gave a wry smile. 'I think my subconscious has been working overtime for months.'

'You're right.' His mouth twisted. 'And now things are beginning to come to the surface. Give it time…and remember that I'm here to help you if there's anything you can't handle. A problem shared, as they say.'

'Thanks, Ben. You've already done so much for me.'

He smiled. 'I think what you need is a day out, a chance to unwind. Perhaps we could take Emily to visit one of the local nature reserves at the weekend.'

'I think she would like that. I would, too.'

His glance meshed with hers. 'Good. That's what we'll do, then.'

At the hospital, they went straight into the A and E department where they were scheduled to be for the rest of the day, and Ben went to liaise with his colleagues about the patient. 'His skin is very cold and pale now,' he said, 'so I think we should give him more epinephrine, but intravenously this time in a dilute solution.'

The other doctor agreed, and the epinephrine was given right away, but there was no reaction. 'Let's try another dose,' Ben's colleague suggested.

The second dose of epinephrine was administered, and a moment later, to the wonder of everyone in the room, the patient opened his eyes. 'What happened to me?' he said, his fingers going to the oxygen mask.

Sarah breathed a sigh of relief and Ben grinned crookedly. 'You're in hospital,' he told the man. 'You were found slumped at the wheel of your car. Can you tell me your name?'

'Martin…Martin Sims.' Sarah noticed that he had developed a slight tremor, and a glance at the monitor showed that his heart rate was very fast. She guessed that was a response to the epinephrine.

'We think you must have had a reaction to something that you've eaten or something that you've come in contact with. Can you think of anything you've had that you wouldn't normally eat or drink?'

Martin shook his head. 'I just had cereal for breakfast, and at lunchtime I picked up a cheeseburger from the corner café, but there's nothing else I can think of. I haven't been feeling too well lately, and the doctor said I had a chest infection, but I didn't want to take time off work. I was on my way back to the office when I started to feel ill, but I thought it would pass because I took the first of my antibiotics with my drink at lunchtime.'

'What antibiotics would they be?' Ben asked. 'We didn't find any tablets or capsules on you.'

'No, I left the bottle at home, and just brought one tablet with me. It was penicillin.'

'Ah…' Ben let out a long sigh and light gleamed in his eyes. 'I think we may have our answer. I imagine that you may well be allergic to penicillin.'

Martin stared at him in shock. 'I didn't know,' he said.

The rest of the day went by smoothly enough, and at the end of his shift Ben drove Sarah back home. They picked up Emily from Carol's house, and as he drove away from the village Ben said, 'Would you like to come straight round to my place and I'll make dinner for us? I thought I might do a quick spaghetti Bolognese. I always make far too much for one, and I would love you to share it with me.'

'Thanks,' Sarah said with a smile. 'That sounds wonderful. It's one of Emily's favourites.'

In his kitchen, he went to find paper and a pencil, along with shapes for Emily to draw round, then he teased the little girl about the fluffy owl on her T-shirt.

'Will he bite me if I touch his beak?' he asked.

'No,' Emily said, laughing. 'He doesn't bite.'

'Are you sure?' He tentatively ran a finger over the owl's fluffy head. 'Ouch!' he said, jumping back. 'He did bite me… Look, he bit my finger. Where's the end of my finger gone?' He hid his index finger from view.

Emily gave him a quizzical look from under her lashes and began to prise his fingers open. ''Tisn't gone. It's there, see?' she said in triumph a moment later.

Ben looked astonished. 'Where?'

'There.' She waggled his finger. 'It's there.'

His eyes widened. 'Well, I never. So it is.'

She giggled. 'Silly Ben. You didn't know where your finger was.'

He laughed with her. 'It's a good thing you're here to find it for me, isn't it?'

Emily was still giggling as she went to sit at the breakfast bar to do her drawing, and Sarah said softly, 'You're the best thing to happen to Emily in a long time. You're so good with her.'

'She's a lovely child. It's easy to get along with Emily.' He started to heat a pan of water for the spaghetti. 'Sit yourself down while I get the food started.' He pointed to a chair.

'I'll help you,' she said, but he shook his head and waved her to the seat.

'Tell me how it felt, being in A and E today. Was there anything that reminded you of how things used to be?'

'I'm not sure.' Her face took on a perplexed expression. 'It all seemed vaguely familiar somehow. I remembered a lot of the procedures, the medicines and the equipment, and I found that I was predicting the course of action the doctors would take.'

She watched him toss onions in a heated pan, and then add minced meat and sauce. 'I was surprised that no one minded me being there. No one seemed to object to me standing by and watching what they were doing.'

He reached for salt and added a pinch to the mix in the pan, then sprinkled herbs over the simmering sauce.

'That smells good,' she murmured. 'Are you sure I can't help?'

'I'm quite sure.' He put plates under the grill to warm. 'I think you'll find that most of the people who work in our A and E department are easygoing and ready to accept newcomers. Anyway, they must have seen you from a distance when we've handed over patients into their care before now.'

'I suppose so.' She frowned. 'I don't think they were all like that where I used to work. I remember someone used to tell me that some people were uptight and picky because they weren't sure of themselves, and they felt threatened by bright young doctors.' She struggled to grasp the elusive threads of memory. 'He was trying to comfort me, I think. He said it didn't matter.'

'He?'

Sarah looked up. Ben had stopped what he was doing and was watching her closely, a cautious, almost vigilant expression on his face.

'I… Yes… I remember there was someone.' She frowned.

'Someone close?'

All at once her throat was aching and her eyes stung with the sudden surge of unspent tears. Why was this happening now? She didn't want this memory, not here, not now, when everything was going so well, when she was here in Ben's home and he was the whole world to her.

'I think so.' The words came out as a whisper, and she wished she could take them back, but he was asking her, and she knew that for both their sakes nothing but the truth would do. 'I'm sorry.'

'Don't be.' His jaw was rigid, as though it was locked in a spasm of regret, and his whole body was still. 'Do you recall anything else about him?'

'I… He said he would come and join me.' She pressed her fingers to her temples as she fought to regain the images and words that flitted in and out of her mind. 'I was going away and he said he would come and be with me.'

Ben pulled air into his lungs and then stiffly turned back to the hob. He didn't say anything more for a long time, but concentrated on preparing the meal, and Sarah wished that there was something she could do to put things right.

To keep busy, and to stop herself from thinking, she began to set the table, laying out cutlery and serviettes.

'There's a bottle of wine in the fridge and glasses in the cupboard over there,' Ben pointed out, glancing over to her as he drained the spaghetti. She nodded and went to fetch them.

'OK, this is ready,' he said a few minutes later. 'Come and tuck in.' He put out plates of spaghetti Bolognese on the table, and then busied himself pouring wine for himself and Sarah.

Sarah watched him and briefly pressed her teeth into her lower lip. He was behaving perfectly normally. It was as though she had never mentioned the man she had worked with in A and E—the man who had felt strongly enough about her that he had said he would come after her when she left. Her mind was in a whirl. Was it possible that he might have been Emily's father?

Emily was still busy drawing her pictures, and Sarah went to bring her over to the table for her food. 'I'll cut up the spaghetti for you,' she said. 'It will be easier for you to manage.'

'I done picture for you, Mummy,' Emily told her, waving the paper under her nose. 'It's a picture of you.'

Sarah studied the pencilled egg shape that had squiggles for eyes and a mouth, with thready arms and legs protruding from the sides. 'That's lovely,' she said. 'What a beautiful picture.'

Emily was clearly pleased with Sarah's comments, and didn't seem at all inclined to go and eat. 'Did you been work today, Mummy?' she asked. 'Carol said you been to work at the hospital. I draw picture of people in their beds.'

'Yes, that's right. I went to see the poorly people.' Sarah gathered up the pencil as Emily would have started on another drawing. 'You can do more later.'

Emily nodded. 'Mummy was poorly in hospital.'

'Yes. But Mummy's getting better now.'

Emily frowned, as though she didn't quite understand, and Sarah said softly, 'See if you can eat your dinner all up. It will help you to grow big and strong.'

'I already strong.' Her eyes grew large. 'I can lift my toy box up.'

'So you are,' said Ben, joining in. 'But Mummy's right. You need to eat up, and then you'll be even stronger.'

'Stronger than Joseph?' Emily thought about that. 'He

pusheded me out of the home corner, so I pusheded him back, and Mrs Pearson told us to stop it.'

Sarah smiled wryly. 'Well, Mrs Pearson was right. Neither of you should have been pushing.'

She looked up at Ben and saw that he, too, was smiling. He picked up his fork and twirled spaghetti around it. Sarah followed his cue and began to eat her meal.

'Perhaps the man in A and E was just a colleague,' she ventured in a low voice after a minute or two. 'In my mind, I can see his face, but there isn't a lot more that comes to mind. Perhaps I didn't remember correctly.'

Ben paused to take a sip of his wine. 'It's possible. I still can't figure out why he didn't actually come and find you. He must have known where you were heading.'

'Maybe.'

For the rest of the meal they talked about other things, about how he was going to search for her parents and the work that they did in A and E, anything rather than dwell on the man who might be part of her life.

'I thought we might go out to the bird sanctuary at the weekend, if that's all right with you,' Ben murmured. 'There aren't just birds there. There's a pet corner as well and a play area for Emily. I think you would both enjoy it.'

Sarah nodded. 'We'll look forward to it.'

After dinner, Sarah helped Ben to clear the dishes away, and settled Emily in the living room in front of the television for a while. A travel programme was being shown, and Emily was entranced by the beach scenes and the seagulls noisily searching for food in the rock pools.

'Your living room is so beautiful,' Sarah told Ben, as they finished sipping their wine in the kitchen. 'The sofas are really comfortable and I love the fabric and the soft patterns. And as to that glass table, I've never seen anything so lovely. It must be unique.'

'My father had it made for us,' he said. 'He was a doctor himself, but he had a creative streak and loved to design things. He had an eye for painting, too, and I have a couple of his landscapes, one in the living room and one in the study. My mother has the rest.'

'He was a very talented artist,' Sarah murmured. She remembered the landscape on the wall of the study. It showed a house overlooking the wide curve of a bay, and in the distance, close to the horizon, there was a sailing ship.

Ben nodded, his mouth curving into a wry grin. 'I often thought that he might make a living from it, but you hear about artists starving in garrets, so it's probably just as well that he stuck with the medical profession.'

Sarah smiled with him, and for a blissful moment, as they stood close together by the French doors, it was as though they were linked by invisible bonds. They were so close to one another that she could feel the warmth coming from him.

Then Emily called out, a shocked cry that instantly had Sarah's attention.

'Mummy…Mummy…' There was an urgency in the child's voice, a note that had to be responded to right away, and Sarah glanced briefly at Ben, sliding her wineglass down onto the table before she hurried out of the kitchen to see what it was that was provoking her child to call out.

Emily was sitting on the carpet, her eyes as wide as could be as she gazed at the television screen.

'What is it, Emily?' Sarah glanced around the living room, not knowing what to expect. 'Why were you shouting?'

'Mummy, look. Come see.' There was a note of agitation in the childish voice.

Sarah came further into the room and sat down on the sofa close by the little girl, aware that Ben had followed and was standing by the door. 'What's the matter?'

Emily didn't answer. Instead, she continued to watch the programme that was being played out on television.

On the screen the camera was following the progress of a yacht as it set out from the harbour. It was a ketch, with a main mast and a shorter mizzen mast aft. On board was a man and a woman, though their faces were out of focus to Sarah.

'Daddy,' Emily said, pointing the finger at the screen. She wagged the finger up and down. Her voice became louder and more excitable as she watched the sailing boat move across the water. 'Daddy on boat. And Mummy.' By now, it wasn't just a finger that was pointing. Her whole hand was extended towards the screen, the fingers splayed out, her concentration intense.

Sarah frowned. 'What do you mean, Emily? They are just people on holiday.' Why would Emily be saying that? 'They can't be your mummy and daddy. I'm your mummy. You know that, don't you? I'm here with you now.'

Months ago the child had watched a traumatic event unfold, seeing Sarah injured. Could it be that she was linking the pictures on the screen with something that played on in her mind?

'Daddy not go on boat again. Not go.' The child glared at the television, and Sarah was at a loss to know what was going on. She glanced across the room at Ben, and her bewilderment must have been clear on her face, but he looked equally baffled.

She turned her attention back to the TV programme, searching for clues as to what had prompted this explosion of anguish on Emily's part. The little girl's expression was fierce, as though the picture on the screen held within it all the bad things that could cause her harm.

'Emily felled down.' She was becoming more and more distressed as she gesticulated towards the television. 'Emily not go in water…never, never.' She sucked in a noisy breath. 'Emily not like wet.'

Sarah watched the sailboat skim across the water, trying to make sense of what Emily was saying and how the programme was linked to it. And suddenly, as the boat began to list to one side as the wind caught its sails, the whole, sorry episode began to unfold in her mind. All at once she knew exactly what was going on in Emily's mind because the sight of the boat and the water triggered something horrifying deep in the recesses of her brain.

'Oh, no…' She gave a shocked gasp. 'No, no…'

'What's wrong, Sarah?' Ben came to stand beside her, a look of concern on his face. 'Have you remembered something?'

She couldn't answer him. She couldn't speak. All she knew was that something dark and awful was unravelling in her mind, a memory was surfacing that she couldn't bear, that she didn't want, and she wished with all her heart that she could push it back from where it had come.

CHAPTER TEN

'SARAH?' Ben was watching her closely, and Sarah gave a shuddery breath, forcing herself to deal with the cold feeling of dread that was closing in on her.

'Emily's right,' she managed, her voice a cracked whisper. Seeing the man at the helm of the boat had brought it all flooding back to her, the whole tragic incident. It shocked her to the core and filled her with despair.

Emily dragged her gaze from the screen and turned to look up at Sarah. Her face crumpled. 'Daddy gone,' she said on a sob. 'Mummy poorly.' She was trembling, and she lifted her arms up to Sarah, as though she alone had the power to make everything right.

Only Sarah didn't know how to do that. She reached for Emily, lifting her onto her knee, and she held her close, but all the while an icy tide was creeping through her veins.

Emily's reaction to the man and woman on the boat had stirred up things that she would rather had stayed hidden, but now it was too late, because the monster was unleashed and there was no escaping it.

She stroked the little girl's hair and tried to make soothing sounds, but deep inside she knew that this was something that could never be made right. It was all coming back to her now with terrible, awful clarity, and tears began to trickle slowly down her cheeks.

She swallowed hard against the lump that formed in her throat. 'I'm here, Emily,' she said huskily. 'You're safe. I won't let you go.'

The little girl buried her head against Sarah's breast. 'Daddy picked me up,' she mumbled, 'but Daddy gone. Mummy gone.'

'I know, Emily. I know.' She kissed the child's temple, and held her tight.

They stayed like that, locked in an embrace, for what seemed like an eternity. Ben crouched down in front of them, looking into Sarah's eyes as he wrapped his arms around both of them.

'You've remembered something, haven't you?' he said as he looked into her stricken eyes.

She nodded and struggled to get her words out against the aching in her throat. 'I wish I hadn't but I can't stop the pictures from coming into my mind.'

She kissed Emily's head, comforting her as best she could until gradually the child's sobs quietened and she became still. After a while it dawned on Sarah that she had fallen asleep in her arms.

She closed her eyes briefly to quell the sting of tears that threatened to run down her face and mingle with the dried streaks of those that had gone before.

'What can I do?' Ben asked. 'Tell me how I can help.'

'No one can help,' she said in a whisper. 'It was awful.' She dragged air shakily into her lungs. 'They both died.'

'Who died?'

'Emily's father and my sister.'

Ben's eyes darkened in shock. 'Do you think you can tell me about it?' He reached out to cover her hands with his. 'How did it happen?'

'Adam…' She tried to still the trembling of her voice. 'Adam hired a boat so that they could go sailing for the afternoon…but later on a gale blew up, and he began to lose control of the yacht. He radioed that he was having trouble with the boat's power, and it turned out that the engine had been overheating and the batteries weren't sufficient to keep up the power supply.'

Her mouth moved in a spasm of painful emotion. 'We learned that from the accident report that was made when the boat was checked over afterwards.'

She stopped for a moment so that she could try to gain control of herself once more. 'Emily was with them, and it seems that she was in danger of going overboard at one point…I think that's what she meant when she said she fell…so Adam secured her to a seat on the boat. But all the while the waves were coming up over the yacht, and he and Rebecca were thrown into the sea.'

She bowed her head as though that would stop her from seeing the images that poured into her mind. 'They were wearing lifejackets, but Adam hit his head on the way down and died from his injuries. The coastguard picked up Rebecca from the sea and found Emily on board, still strapped to the seat. She was safe, but she was soaking wet and very cold.'

Ben was watching her face intently. 'How do you know all this?'

'I know it because…' She stopped as tears filled her eyes. 'Because Rebecca clung to life for a few days. She was in the water so long that she was suffering from hypothermia when they eventually brought her out. They took her to hospital, but she was so cold that it took hours to revive her. When she finally regained consciousness, she seemed to rally a little, and we thought that she was going to survive. Over the next day or so she even managed to tell us something of what had happened.'

She swallowed hard and clasped her hands more firmly around Emily, holding onto the one precious thing she had left from that awful time. 'Then she started to show signs of pneumonia and the doctors did everything they could to try to pull her through, but it was no use. In her weakened state she wasn't able to fight it. She never recovered.'

Ben came and sat on the sofa beside her, folding her into his arms. 'I'm so sorry.' He drew her against him, simply holding her, and for a long time they were silent, with Sarah taking comfort from his nearness.

When she stirred a while later, he said softly, 'Rebecca was your sister?'

Sarah nodded. 'She was older than me. I thought the world of her.'

'I don't think I understand this,' he said with a puzzled frown. 'You said that Emily was out with your sister on the boat. Why weren't you with them?'

Sarah drew in a shaky breath. 'That's just it. I wasn't part of the family group. You see, I realise now that I'm not Emily's mother at all. She was Adam and Rebecca's daughter.'

He gave a sharp intake of breath. 'You're not her mother? How can that be?' He shook his head. 'I'm having a lot of trouble taking this in. I never imagined for a moment that you weren't her natural mother. You're both so alike in looks…

your hair colour, your eyes. There must be some mistake. Are you sure you have this right? Do you think your memory could be playing tricks on you?'

'No.' Her mouth made a sombre line. 'I'm having trouble accepting it as well. Ever since my head injury I've believed that she was mine, because everyone told me that it was so, and I've loved her deeply, even though I couldn't ever remember having a child. It never occurred to me that they had it wrong. We have such a bond between us, and it's hard for me to acknowledge that she isn't my very own flesh and blood. But now I have to come to terms with the truth because some things have come back to me with absolute clarity.' She hesitated. 'I remember my sister asking me…to take care of her.' Her voice broke on the words.

'I'm sorry, Sarah.' Ben cupped her face in his hands. 'This has all been a tremendous shock to you, to discover what really went on, and it's no wonder that you were traumatised by what happened. It must have been terrible to have to accept that the people you loved had gone out of your life, and that Emily was left without a family.'

She nodded. 'At first none of us knew quite what to do. I was working full time, and my father and mother weren't living in the country. My father was reorganising an overseas branch of the company, and my mother was working with him as an interpreter. Adam's parents were long since gone, and that meant that initially I was the only one on hand to deal with everything. Of course, my parents came home as soon as they heard about the accident.'

Her mouth made an awkward shape as she tried to counter the grief that suddenly welled up in her. 'We had to think about what to do for the best for Emily.'

'But in the end you must have decided to keep her with you.'

'Yes, that's right.' She frowned, trying to recall the exact circumstances. 'My mother wanted to help out with Emily, but she has a job that takes her overseas quite often. She would have given it up, but in those first few months Emily clung to me and wouldn't be consoled if I left her for any length of time. I had some leave due to me, so I used that in order to take care of her. I think we came to some kind of agreement in the end that I would keep her with me and my parents would help out whenever they were back home.'

She thought about it for a moment longer, trying to piece everything together in her mind. 'Some things are still a bit shrouded in fog,' she told him. 'It's difficult to recall exactly, but I know that I stayed for some time in Rebecca's house because I didn't want to disturb Emily any more than was necessary.'

'Did something go wrong? What was it that caused you to leave? Do you know?'

'I think it was all too much for me. I expect I was trying to keep down a full-time job in A and E, but it must have been hard, looking after Emily as well. I'm pretty sure that I adopted her, because I remember signing lots of forms and there was some kind of assessment, but in the end I must have decided to give up my job and move up to the Peak District. Perhaps I was going to work part time. I can't remember exactly what I had in mind.'

She looked at him, her whole body shaky in the aftermath of this discovery. 'It's all a bit patchy, still. Bits of it are very clear, almost more so than I can bear, but the rest of it is hazy.' She frowned, thinking things through, and suddenly became very still.

'Are you all right?' Ben's expression was full of concern.

'My name—' she said, her eyes widening '—it's just come back to me…' She broke off, overwhelmed by the shock of this new discovery. 'It's not Hall, that was my sister's married name. My name is Marshall, Sarah Marshall.' She laid a hand on his arm, as though she was reaching out to him, wanting something that she couldn't put into words. 'But I still can't remember where my parents were living.'

'I'm sure that will come back to you, with time. I expect you were on your way to their house when you were attacked. They must be desperate to know what happened to you, but now we have your real name we stand a good chance of being able to track them down.'

She leaned against him, drinking in the comfort of his strong body, and he drew her head into the hollow of his shoulder, stroking her hair and laying a gentle kiss on her forehead.

He was quiet for a while and then he asked, 'Did Adam work at the hospital with you? Could he have been saying at some point that he was going to come and see you where you were living? Perhaps he and Rebecca were going to visit you before the accident happened?'

Sarah shook her head. 'No. He worked as a sports instructor. That's how he came to have a love of sailing and all things outdoors.' Her voice broke. 'Rebecca was perfect for him. Before Emily was born she worked as a physiotherapist, and she helped rehabilitate people with sports injuries.'

He ran his hand gently down her arm. 'This has been a lot for you to take in. Why don't you and Emily stay here for the night? I don't think it would be good for you to be on your own, and I could get the spare bedroom ready for you. Emily could have the put-you-up bed next to yours, and then if she wakes up in the night, you will be there for her.'

She looked up at him. 'Thanks. I'd like that. I really appreciate everything that you're doing for me.' She reached up and touched his face, running her fingers over his cheek. 'I don't know how I would have coped without you.'

'I'll help you to get through this,' he said. He frowned. 'Emily will need a lot of help, too, but in a way it's good that she has been able to tell you what happened. It means that you can talk to her about it and help her through any worries she might have. Children cope much better than we imagine, and in a while this will be all in the past for her.'

'Yes, there is that. Somehow I'm going to have to help her to lose her fear of water and boats, too. That's going to take some doing.'

'Maybe, but she's a bright, lively little girl, and I'm sure we'll find a way.'

Sarah clung on to that word 'we'. It was such a small word, but it meant so much. Ben had told her that he would be by her side through all this, and she knew that she could rely on him. She also knew that he was haunted by the fact that there was still someone out there who might be looking for her…the man that she had worked with in A and E.

It grieved her that she couldn't set the record straight. Why could she not remember anything about him? Why was her mind such a patchwork of memories?

For now, though, she didn't want to dwell on that. There were other, more immediate concerns.

She did as Ben had suggested, and she and Emily stayed the night in his house, and in the morning she woke to the smell of fresh coffee and toast, filtering up the stairs from the kitchen.

'Emily, sunbeam, it's time for us to get up. You need to get ready for nursery.'

Emily yawned and rubbed her eyes. Then she sat up and looked around, taking in the strange surroundings. It was a pretty room, decorated in soft colours of pink and grey, with dashes of pale blue here and there. The carpet underfoot was thick and luxurious, and across the room the dressing-table was laid out with a selection of toiletries, hand lotion and suncream, along with a brush and comb and a delicate vase with scented rosebuds that filled the air with their perfume.

'Where my teddy bear?' Emily asked.

Sarah looked around. 'There he is, on the floor,' she said. 'You must have pushed him out of bed in the night.'

'Poor Teddy!' Emily exclaimed, reaching down to pick him up and rain kisses over his face. She cuddled the bear, and then put her arms out to Sarah. 'Love you, Mummy,' she said.

Sarah swept her up into her arms. 'Love you, too, loads and loads.' She kissed her and then said, 'Are you going to get washed and dressed, or shall I tickle you?' She raised a hand and pretended that she was about to tickle the little girl.

Emily squealed happily and wriggled in her arms. 'Not tickle, not tickle.'

Sarah set her gently down on the floor once more. 'Are you sure?' She wriggled her fingers and pretended to swoop, and Emily ran, giggling, into the adjoining bathroom.

The next few days passed easily enough, without anything untoward happening. Emily was her usual happy self, and whenever Sarah or Ben carefully brought up the subject of boats or her parents, she answered them solemnly and appeared to have accepted what had happened in the past. Perhaps her recent experience had been cathartic, and the worst was over for her now.

At the weekend Ben drove them to the bird sanctuary, as he had promised. It was a beautiful summer's day, with a clear blue sky, and the countryside was in full bloom. Emily was singing softly to herself as they drove along, and Sarah was calm, looking forward to the day ahead.

When they arrived at the sanctuary, Ben lifted Emily onto his shoulders and slipped an arm around Sarah's waist. She loved that familiar contact, and more than anything she wished that she could tell him how much she cared for him, but caution held her back.

She didn't know whether there was someone waiting for her. She might have been married, or even engaged and planning a wedding, and though she had no feelings for anyone in the world but Ben, she had to keep in mind that her past was still uncertain. With all her being, she wanted nothing more than to be with Ben, but how could she do that and risk hurting this other man if he had feelings for her and she had simply cut him out of her life because of a head injury?

'Did you see that?' Emily said, raising her brows. 'The owl turned his head right round. Did you see? Look, he's doing it again.'

'Perhaps he wanted to get a better look at you,' Ben suggested.

'I can't turn my head right round,' Emily said with a frown, straining to twist her head. 'Funny bird.'

They walked around the sanctuary, taking the leafy pathways through the woodland and talking to Emily about the animals they saw. Sarah pointed out the sleek coats of the otters as they swam through the water, and the child watched in fascination.

'Look,' she said in wonder, 'there's a baby otter. He's all furry.'

'He's beautiful,' Sarah agreed.

They stopped for lunch, sitting at a wooden bench table outside the cafeteria, and Sarah breathed in the warm country air, sitting close to Ben while they watched Emily play on the grass with the other children.

He put his arm around her and she snuggled against him, giving in to temptation and trying to persuade herself that it wasn't wrong to feel this way.

Some half an hour later they set off to find the pets' corner, where Emily stroked the rabbits and guinea pigs and fed food pellets to the goats. Nearby there was a pond, and a family of ducks was swimming across the surface. Sarah broke up some bread left over from lunch and gave it to Emily so that she could throw it to them.

'Gobble, gobble...quack, quack,' Emily shouted gleefully as the ducks accepted her offerings. Laughing, she came back to Ben and Sarah.

'Has all the bread gone?' Ben said.

She nodded.

'Then it's probably time that we started for home.'

'OK.' A goat wandered across the paddock and started nudging Emily's leg. She tried to pat him on the head then looked at Sarah. 'Can we take the goat home? It could stay in our garden and eat the grass.'

Sarah rolled her eyes heavenward. 'How am I going to get out of that one?' she muttered to Ben.

He laughed. 'Now, that's tricky.'

'I think he might do more than eat the grass,' Sarah said in a thoughtful tone, turning her attention back to the child.

'I've heard that goats eat lots of things, and we wouldn't want to see him eat your toys, or try to eat your dress, would we?'

Emily wrapped her dress closely round herself and shook her head vigorously. 'Him not eat my dress.' She wagged finger at the animal. 'Bad goat.' She started to move away from him, positioning herself alongside Sarah as they walked back to where they had parked the car.

'Well, that was easy enough,' Ben said with a smile.

He drove them back to Sarah's cottage, going into the house with them when Sarah invited him to stay a while. Emily ran to play with her doll's house in a corner of the living room, while Sarah rummaged in the fridge for cold drinks.

She set them out on a tray with a jug and glass tumblers and carried it through to the room where Emily was playing.

'I've had a lovely day,' she said, placing the tray down on a table and turning to look at Ben. She let her hand glide over his arm. 'Thank you for taking us out.'

'I'm glad that you enjoyed it. It's good to see you smiling and happy.' He moved towards her, his hands lightly cupping her shoulders, and for a long moment she thought that he would take her in his arms and kiss her. She found herself longing for the touch of his lips on hers, but the wait seemed endless.

He gazed down at her, his eyes intent on her face, but though he drew her near him and stood poised, his lips just a fraction of a breath away from hers, he resisted, closing his eyes, and it seemed as though he was fighting a battle for control of himself. Neither one of them moved.

Then the phone rang, and Sarah almost jumped with surprise. She frowned, gathering herself together.

'I wonder who that can be? I'm not expecting anyone to

ring and, as far as I know, Carol is out for the day.' A thought occurred to her. 'Unless it's your mother, of course. Perhaps she's been trying to get in touch with you and couldn't get through for some reason.'

Ben looked mystified. 'I can't think why she would need to do that.'

Sarah went over to the table by the sofa and picked up the receiver. It wasn't Ben's mother on the phone, but as she listened to the man who was speaking, her mouth dropped open in startled wonder. She recognised that voice. She knew who it was.

'Is that Sarah?' he asked. 'I've been given your number, and I'm not sure if I'm speaking to the right person.'

'Yes,' she said huskily. 'That's right. I'm Sarah.'

She heard a heavy, shuddery sigh come from the receiver. 'Thank heaven,' the man said. 'I've been calling all afternoon in the hope that I would find you.'

'I've been out. I had no idea that you knew how to get in touch. How did you find me after all this time?' She saw that Ben had tensed suddenly, and she realised that he must be wondering who was on the other end of the line. She spoke hurriedly into the phone. 'Can you just hold on for a moment? I need to speak to someone. It's really important.'

'All right. Of course.'

She reached out for Ben. 'It's my father,' she said. 'I knew his voice as soon as I heard him speak.' She slipped her arm around his waist and pressed herself against the warmth of his body. Then she put the phone to her ear once more and said, 'It's so good to hear you. I had no idea where you were. How did you find me?'

'My boss said that someone was trying to put you in touch

with me. Your mother and I—we didn't know what had happened. We kept phoning our old house—you were supposed to be living there—but no one answered, and the neighbours hadn't any idea where you might be.'

He seemed to be having trouble getting his words out, and she guessed that he was as overwhelmed as she was. He paused for a moment to get his breath. 'When we didn't hear from you, we contacted the hospital where you used to work, but they said that you had left as planned. They didn't know what had happened to you. We put the police onto it, but they had no luck finding you. Thank heaven you're safe.'

He broke off, and Sarah could hear a conversation going on in the background. A moment later he said, 'It's your mother. She's desperate to speak to you.' He was laughing now, and Sarah couldn't stop a smile from coming over her face as her mother came on the line.

'Sarah, is that you?'

'Yes, it's me.'

'After all this time,' her mother said breathlessly. 'You can't imagine how worried we've been. We've tried everything to find you, and then your father's boss told us that you had been hurt and that you had lost your memory, and I was so afraid that you still wouldn't know who we were. I can't wait to get back and see you.'

Sarah tried to get a word in edgeways, but her mother was still in full flow. 'And how is Emily? Is she all right? Are you managing to cope with looking after her? I never wanted to leave the country in the first place. I knew it was a mistake. I should have stayed behind with you, then none of this would have happened.'

'Mother,' Sarah said, chuckling, 'everything is fine, just

wonderful. It's so good to hear from you. When are you coming home?'

'In a couple of weeks. Your father's work over here will be finished then, and he'll be back at his old place.'

'That's good.' Sarah looked across at Ben to see if he was following this conversation. He nodded, and she sent him a quick grin. 'I'm so looking forward to seeing you both.'

'It can't come too soon,' her mother said. 'By the way, we had a call some time ago from Jason. Do you remember Jason?'

'Yes, I do, I remember him.' Sarah felt Ben stiffen, and she ran her hand along his side and sent him a reassuring glance, saying, 'It's all right, Ben. It's all come back to me.'

Her mother was frowning. Sarah knew it because she could hear it in the words that her mother said. 'Who is that you're talking to? Is that young man with you the one who got in touch with your father's boss?'

'You mean Ben?'

'Yes, Ben. That's the one. If it hadn't been for him, we would never have found you. Tell him thank you, thank you, thank you so much.'

Sarah sent Ben a quick look, her eyebrows raised questioningly. He nodded.

'He heard. He's smiling.' Sarah laughed, and then said, 'You were telling me about Jason phoning you. What was that all about?'

'He was trying to get in touch with you as well,' her mother said. 'Apparently, when you left the hospital where you were working, he told you that he would come and visit you when his contract came to an end. He was planning on getting a job in one of the hospitals in Derbyshire, but he was offered something better down in Kent. I think he just wanted to look you up and make sure that you were managing all right but, like us, he couldn't find you.'

'I don't suppose he left a number with you, did he, or the name of the hospital where he was going to be working?'

'He gave me the name of the hospital. I'm sure he'll be relieved to know that you're OK.'

Sarah sensed that her mother was about to get back into full flow, but she was conscious of Emily tugging at her jeans and she said quickly, 'Would you like to have a word with Emily? She's right here by my side.'

'Oh, yes, yes, please…put her on.'

Sarah looked down at the little girl. 'Nana and Grandad are on the phone. Would you like to talk to them?'

Emily nodded solemnly and Sarah handed her the phone. 'Just say hello, and they'll talk to you,' she said.

Turning back to Ben, Sarah smiled up at him. 'All the pieces are falling into place now. I remember that I used to work with Jason in A and E. We were very close, we even got engaged, but after a while we both realised that we weren't really suited. The relationship wasn't working that well for either of us, but we stayed good friends. Jason helped me through the bad times when I first started looking after Emily.'

She reached up to him and planted a kiss on his mouth, and Ben blinked and kissed her in return. 'What was that for?' he asked, his mouth tilting at the corners.

'For being you, for being here with me and Emily. For everything.'

He kissed her again, and she clung to him, her lips parting beneath his, her whole body alive with the knowledge that this was the best thing that had ever happened to her.

After a while he broke off the kiss, and she realised that the thudding feeling on her thigh was Emily banging the phone against her leg. 'We finished talking,' Emily said. 'I pressed the button and they weren't there any more.'

Sarah began to laugh and clapped a hand to her mouth. 'She must have cut them off,' she said, looking at Ben. 'Not to worry. I expect they'll ring back before too long.' She glanced down at Emily. 'It's a good job the phone will store their number for me. Did you enjoy talking to Nana and Grandad?'

Emily beamed. 'Yes. They're coming home soon, and they're going to bring me a present.' She pressed her hands together in joyful expectation, and then said, 'I go play with my dolly's house.'

'All right.'

Ben still had his arms around her but now he said in a cautious voice, 'You were telling me about Jason, and from the sound of things you're planning on getting in touch with him. Are you sure that you're not still in love with him?'

She shook her head. 'I just want to let him know that I'm all right. We were going to stay in contact with one another just because we were friends. I might have thought that I was in love with him at one time, but that was a long while ago, and it was definitely before I discovered what real love was all about.'

'And what is that?'

She looked into his eyes. 'It's the doctor next door. He's everything I could ever want, and I couldn't bear to think of him not being there.'

He drew her against him, and she loved the way that her soft curves were crushed against his long body. 'You don't know how I've longed for you to say that,' he said on a ragged breath. 'I want to be with you for always. I love you, Sarah. You and Emily both.'

He kissed her with all the pent-up passion of the months that had gone before, blotting out all the worry and uncertainty that had beleaguered her all that time. It was a warm, wonderful kiss that fired her blood and sent ripples of sensation to every nerve ending in her body. Sarah wanted that moment to go on for ever and ever.

It wasn't to be, though, because in a little while they both became aware of small hands clutching at them, one little curled fist tugging at Ben's shirt. They looked down.

'What you doing?' Emily was frowning as she stared at Ben. 'Is you kissing my mummy?'

'Yes. That's right,' Ben answered soberly.

Emily thought about that for a while. 'Is you going to be my new daddy?'

The question was so overwhelming in its simplicity that both Ben and Sarah felt for the sofa behind them and sat down.

'Yes, I'd like that, very much,' Ben told her. 'Would that be all right?'

Emily nodded. 'Yes.' She frowned. 'Are you going to kiss my mummy again?'

'I thought I might.' He studied her momentarily. 'What do you think about that?'

She scrunched up her nose and gave an awkward kind of shrug. 'It's all right, I suppose.'

Ben reached for her and drew her up on to their laps so that she was sitting between them. They both held her close. 'We both love you, Emily,' he said, 'and we want to be your mummy and daddy. That would be good, wouldn't it?'

'Yes.' Emily gave a contented sigh. She leaned back against them and basked in their cuddles.

Over the top of her head, Ben sought out Sarah's lips once more, and flame ran through her, searing her from head to toe as he kissed her long and hard. After a while he reluctantly broke off the kiss.

'Will you marry me, Sarah?' he asked in a thickened voice.

'Oh, yes,' Sarah murmured, reaching for him once more and kissing him in the full knowledge that she had come home at last. 'Yes, please.'

MILLS & BOON
Pure reading pleasure

AUGUST 2008 HARDBACK TITLES

ROMANCE

Virgin for the Billionaire's Taking   978 0 263 20334 9
Penny Jordan
Purchased: His Perfect Wife *Helen Bianchin*   978 0 263 20335 6
The Vasquez Mistress *Sarah Morgan*   978 0 263 20336 3
At the Sheikh's Bidding *Chantelle Shaw*   978 0 263 20337 0
The Spaniard's Marriage Bargain *Abby Green*   978 0 263 20338 7
Sicilian Millionaire, Bought Bride   978 0 263 20339 4
Catherine Spencer
Italian Prince, Wedlocked Wife *Jennie Lucas*   978 0 263 20340 0
The Desert King's Pregnant Bride *Annie West*   978 0 263 20341 7
Bride at Briar's Ridge *Margaret Way*   978 0 263 20342 4
Last-Minute Proposal *Jessica Hart*   978 0 263 20343 1
The Single Mum and the Tycoon   978 0 263 20344 8
Caroline Anderson
Found: His Royal Baby *Raye Morgan*   978 0 263 20345 5
The Millionaire's Nanny Arrangement   978 0 263 20346 2
Linda Goodnight
Hired: The Boss's Bride *Ally Blake*   978 0 263 20347 9
A Boss Beyond Compare *Dianne Drake*   978 0 263 20348 6
The Emergency Doctor's Chosen Wife   978 0 263 20349 3
Molly Evans

HISTORICAL

Scandalising the Ton *Diane Gaston*   978 0 263 20207 6
Her Cinderella Season *Deb Marlowe*   978 0 263 20208 3
The Warrior's Princess Bride *Meriel Fuller*   978 0 263 20209 0

MEDICAL™

A Baby for Eve *Maggie Kingsley*   978 0 263 19906 2
Marrying the Millionaire Doctor *Alison Roberts*   978 0 263 19907 9
His Very Special Bride *Joanna Neil*   978 0 263 19908 6
City Surgeon, Outback Bride *Lucy Clark*   978 0 263 19909 3

MILLS & BOON™

Pure reading pleasure™

AUGUST 2008 LARGE PRINT TITLES

ROMANCE

The Italian Billionaire's Pregnant Bride *Lynne Graham*	978 0 263 20066 9
The Guardian's Forbidden Mistress *Miranda Lee*	978 0 263 20067 6
Secret Baby, Convenient Wife *Kim Lawrence*	978 0 263 20068 3
Caretti's Forced Bride *Jennie Lucas*	978 0 263 20069 0
The Bride's Baby *Liz Fielding*	978 0 263 20070 6
Expecting a Miracle *Jackie Braun*	978 0 263 20071 3
Wedding Bells at Wandering Creek *Patricia Thayer*	978 0 263 20072 0
The Loner's Guarded Heart *Michelle Douglas*	978 0 263 20073 7

HISTORICAL

Lady Gwendolen Investigates *Anne Ashley*	978 0 263 20163 5
The Unknown Heir *Anne Herries*	978 0 263 20164 2
Forbidden Lord *Helen Dickson*	978 0 263 20165 9

MEDICAL™

The Doctor's Bride By Sunrise *Josie Metcalfe*	978 0 263 19968 0
Found: A Father For Her Child *Amy Andrews*	978 0 263 19969 7
A Single Dad at Heathermere *Abigail Gordon*	978 0 263 19970 3
Her Very Special Baby *Lucy Clark*	978 0 263 19971 0
The Heart Surgeon's Secret Son *Janice Lynn*	978 0 263 19972 7
The Sheikh Surgeon's Proposal *Olivia Gates*	978 0 263 19973 4

en Std HB

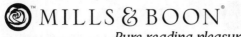

MILLS & BOON®
Pure reading pleasure™

SEPTEMBER 2008 HARDBACK TITLES

ROMANCE

Ruthlessly Bedded by the Italian Billionaire *Emma Darcy*	978 0 263 20350 9
Mendez's Mistress *Anne Mather*	978 0 263 20351 6
Rafael's Suitable Bride *Cathy Williams*	978 0 263 20352 3
Desert Prince, Defiant Virgin *Kim Lawrence*	978 0 263 20353 0
Sicilian Husband, Unexpected Baby *Sharon Kendrick*	978 0 263 20354 7
Hired: The Italian's Convenient Mistress *Carol Marinelli*	978 0 263 20355 4
Antonides' Forbidden Wife *Anne McAllister*	978 0 263 20356 1
The Millionaire's Chosen Bride *Susanne James*	978 0 263 20357 8
Wedded in a Whirlwind *Liz Fielding*	978 0 263 20358 5
Blind Date with the Boss *Barbara Hannay*	978 0 263 20359 2
The Tycoon's Christmas Proposal *Jackie Braun*	978 0 263 20360 8
Christmas Wishes, Mistletoe Kisses *Fiona Harper*	978 0 263 20361 5
Rescued by the Magic of Christmas *Melissa McClone*	978 0 263 20362 2
Her Millionaire, His Miracle *Myrna Mackenzie*	978 0 263 20363 9
Italian Doctor, Sleigh-Bell Bride *Sarah Morgan*	978 0 263 20364 6
The Desert Surgeon's Secret Son *Olivia Gates*	978 0 263 20365 3

HISTORICAL

Scandalous Secret, Defiant Bride *Helen Dickson*	978 0 263 20210 6
A Question of Impropriety *Michelle Styles*	978 0 263 20211 3
Conquering Knight, Captive Lady *Anne O'Brien*	978 0 263 20212 0

MEDICAL™

Dr Devereux's Proposal *Margaret McDonagh*	978 0 263 19910 9
Children's Doctor, Meant-to-be Wife *Meredith Webber*	978 0 263 19911 6
Christmas at Willowmere *Abigail Gordon*	978 0 263 19912 3
Dr Romano's Christmas Baby *Amy Andrews*	978 0 263 19913 0

MILLS & BOON®

Pure reading pleasure™

SEPTEMBER 2008 LARGE PRINT TITLES

ROMANCE

The Markonos Bride *Michelle Reid*	978 0 263 20074 4
The Italian's Passionate Revenge *Lucy Gordon*	978 0 263 20075 1
The Greek Tycoon's Baby Bargain *Sharon Kendrick*	978 0 263 20076 8
Di Cesare's Pregnant Mistress *Chantelle Shaw*	978 0 263 20077 5
His Pregnant Housekeeper *Caroline Anderson*	978 0 263 20078 2
The Italian Playboy's Secret Son *Rebecca Winters*	978 0 263 20079 9
Her Sheikh Boss *Carol Grace*	978 0 263 20080 5
Wanted: White Wedding *Natasha Oakley*	978 0 263 20081 2

HISTORICAL

The Last Rake In London *Nicola Cornick*	978 0 263 20166 6
The Outrageous Lady Felsham *Louise Allen*	978 0 263 20167 3
An Unconventional Miss *Dorothy Elbury*	978 0 263 20168 0

MEDICAL™

The Surgeon's Fatherhood Surprise *Jennifer Taylor*	978 0 263 19974 1
The Italian Surgeon Claims His Bride *Alison Roberts*	978 0 263 19975 8
Desert Doctor, Secret Sheikh *Meredith Webber*	978 0 263 19976 5
A Wedding in Warragurra *Fiona Lowe*	978 0 263 19977 2
The Firefighter and the Single Mum *Laura Iding*	978 0 263 19978 9
The Nurse's Little Miracle *Molly Evans*	978 0 263 19979 6